BOUND FOR DANGER

READ ALL THE MYSTERIES IN THE

HARDY BOYS ADVENTURES:

#1 *Secret of the Red Arrow*

#2 *Mystery of the Phantom Heist*

#3 *The Vanishing Game*

#4 *Into Thin Air*

#5 *Peril at Granite Peak*

#6 *The Battle of Bayport*

#7 *Shadows at Predator Reef*

#8 *Deception on the Set*

#9 *The Curse of the Ancient Emerald*

#10 *Tunnel of Secrets*

#11 *Showdown at Widow Creek*

#12 *The Madman of Black Bear Mountain*

COMING SOON:

#14 *Attack of the Bayport Beast*

#13 BOUND FOR DANGER

FRANKLIN W. DIXON

ALADDIN New York London Toronto Sydney New Delhi

ALADDIN
An imprint of Simon & Schuster Children's Publishing Division
1230 Avenue of the Americas, New York, NY 10020
This Aladdin paperback edition October 2016

Also available in an Aladdin hardcover edition.

Cover designed by Karin Paprocki
Interior designed by Mike Rosamilia
The text of this book was set in Adobe Caslon Pro.
Manufactured in the United States of America 0916 OFF
2 4 6 8 10 9 7 5 3 1
Library of Congress Control Number 2015958999
ISBN 978-1-4814-6832-9 (hc)
ISBN 978-1-4814-6831-2 (pbk)
ISBN 978-1-4814-6833-6 (eBook)

CONTENTS

1

A CAPELLA DREAMS

FRANK

**AVE YOU EVER HAD A DREAM?**

A dream that was worth risking it all? Putting yourself in uncomfortable situations? Facing your fears?

I had that dream. But I'd only recently discovered it.

Three weeks ago, I joined the Bayport High B-Sharps, an a cappella singing group. That's right. *A cappella.* I know most people picture dorky guys in cardigans singing yet another goofy version of Billy Joel's "The Longest Time," but the B-Sharps aren't like that. For one thing, we don't wear cardigans. For another, our captain, Max Crandal, has a strict "no Billy Joel" policy. (It's not that we have anything against Billy Joel, personally. It's just the cliché of the thing.)

And so here I was, heart pounding in my chest, sweaty fists clenched in my pockets. I was about to make my debut with the B-Sharps, performing "The Lion Sleeps Tonight" at a freshman antibullying assembly. I wasn't totally sure what the connection was, topic-wise. All I knew was that I had a solo: *In the village, the peaceful village, the lion . . .*

"How are you doing, Frank?" Max walked up to me and patted me on the back. We were in the wings of the stage, waiting for the Bayport High Improv Group to finish up a sketch, and then we were up.

"I'm good, I'm totally good," I lied. The truth was I was *freaking out*, but I was determined to conquer my fears.

"You really killed it in rehearsal yesterday," Max said with a sincere smile. "I'm sure you'll do great."

I smiled back and thanked him. Max is a stand-up guy, a great captain. He was part of why I was enjoying my time with the B-Sharps so much.

I turned back to the sketch that was wrapping up onstage. The girl playing the person being bullied was being very open and honest about how the bullying made her feel, and the bully was talking about how problems at home were making her act out. My palms started sweating even harder. *Oh God, we're up in, like, one . . .*

"Frank Hardy?"

I turned around, surprised. I'd been so focused on the skit that I hadn't noticed someone walking up behind me. Now I looked down at Seth Diller, Bayport High's own amateur filmmaker, president of the school's AV club, and a vague acquaintance.

"Principal Gerther wants to see you," he said, flashing an official pink request form. When you got one of those, you had to report to the office immediately.

"What does Principal Gerther want?" I asked. It still felt a little weird to refer to him that way. For most of my high school career, he'd been the low-level coach who oversaw study hall. But then my brother Joe and I had found the acting principal to be involved in some pretty serious shenanigans, and Gerther was promoted.

Seth shrugged. "It's not my job to ask why," he said, waving the form. "It's my job to come and get you, okay? I'm just a messenger."

The skit was finishing up now.

"Can it wait five minutes? I have a part in the next song." I gestured around to my a cappella amigos.

Seth shook his head. "If you look at the form," he said in an annoyed tone, tapping an *X* on the pink paper, "it says right here, 'VERY URGENT.' That means no waiting, no bathroom breaks, no stopping at your locker. We need to go *now*."

I glanced back at Seth. "But . . ."

Max stepped forward. The skit had ended and the improv kids were shuffling backstage. "It's all right, Frank," he said. "Whatever Gerther needs you for, it must be important. Go ahead, we can cover for you."

I sighed, hesitating. I didn't *want* to go. I wanted to kill it during my solo!

Seth waved the form at me again. "Gerther said if we're not back in ten minutes, we both get detention," he said. "I don't know what this is about, but it must be serious."

Great, I thought. "All right, all right," I said, beckoning in front of me. "Lead the way, Seth. I'm sorry, Max."

"No worries." Max shook his head like I shouldn't give it another thought. He really is the nicest guy. "I just hope it all works out."

With a wave to the others, I scurried off to follow Seth, who was already halfway down the aisle to the auditorium entrance. He didn't slow down when he saw I was following him, and I ended up practically running after him the whole way to the office.

Where I found my brother, Joe, waiting. He cocked his eyebrows in surprise when he saw me. *Hmmmm.* If Joe and I were both being called in, that narrowed down the possible topics. To one.

Joe and I aren't perfect students, but we're not the types to get urgently called into the principal's office that often either. And if Gerther wanted to talk to the two of us together, it pretty much had to be about our sleuthing hobby.

"What do you think this is about?" Joe whispered to me when I sat down in a hard plastic chair beside him. Seth dropped off the URGENT pink form with the receptionist, then disappeared into the mailroom.

"I don't know," I admitted. "We haven't worked a case in a few weeks."

Before we could theorize much further, Principal Gerther's door opened and he nodded at us, shouting, "HARDY BOYS? GOOD. COME IN, PLEASE!"

Principal Gerther lost something like 80 percent of his hearing fighting in Vietnam. He yells everything, and doesn't quite understand when people don't yell back.

Joe and I stood and wandered into his office.

"HAVE A SEAT," he barked, settling into his fancy office chair. As Joe and I sat, I noticed that Gerther had pulled out our encyclopedia-size permanent files, and they were sitting on his desk in front of him.

"SO," said Joe, smiling a friendly smile, and affecting the 50 percent volume increase necessary to communicate with our principal. "IS EVERYTHING OKAY? FRANK AND I WERE A BIT SURPRISED TO BE CALLED IN TODAY."

Principal Gerther nodded impatiently. "YES, SURE. EVERYTHING IS FINE, BOYS, BUT I'VE BEEN LOOKING OVER YOUR TRANSCRIPTS." He gestured to the huge files in front of him. "I COULDN'T HELP NOTING THAT THERE'S A LACK OF EXTRACURRICULAR ACTIVITIES."

I looked at Joe in surprise. *What?*

Coach Gerther pointed a chubby finger at us. "YOU'RE GOING TO BE APPLYING TO COLLEGE SOON," he said, "OR AT LEAST FRANK WILL. YOU MUST KNOW HOW COMPETITIVE IT IS NOW. RESPECTABLE GRADES AREN'T ENOUGH TO GET INTO THE TOP SCHOOLS!"

Joe and I frowned at each other. "I know that," I began, "but, ah . . ."

"SPEAK UP, BOY!"

"I PLAY BASEBALL!" Joe shouted. "IN THE SPRING! WE'RE BOTH INVOLVED IN THE GREEN ENVIRONMENTAL CONSERVATION CLUB. AND BESIDES THAT, OUR TIME IS KIND OF TAKEN UP WITH . . . UM . . ."

"EXTRACURRICULAR ACTIVITIES," I put in, "THAT ARE SORT OF . . . WELL . . . OFF THE BOOKS?"

Sleuthing, I tried to tell Principal Gerther telepathically. I wasn't sure how much he knew about our continuing detective work or how he felt about it, so I didn't want to bring it up before he did.

But he was waving his hand dismissively. "THOSE AREN'T ENOUGH," he said.

Suddenly I remembered something that made me sort of righteously indignant. Somehow this led to me raising my hand.

"YES?" Gerther asked, looking a tad annoyed.

"I JOINED THE B-SHARPS A CAPPELLA GROUP!" I shouted defensively. "AND WE WERE JUST

GOING TO HAVE OUR FIRST CONCERT WHEN I GOT CALLED OUT TO COME HERE!"

Principal Gerther looked at me like he smelled something bad. "A CAPPELLA?" he yelled. "THOSE BOYS IN CARDIGANS WHO SING THE FOUR SEASONS SONGS? NO." He looked down at a piece of paper on his desk and shoved it across to us. "I'M TALKING ABOUT REAL EXTRACURRICULAR ACTIVITIES, BOYS. I'VE TAKEN THE LIBERTY OF SIGNING YOU BOTH UP FOR THE VARSITY BASKETBALL TEAM."

Wha . . .? I glanced at Joe. *Is he serious?*

Joe looked as startled as I felt. "UM," he said, looking down at the paper, which looked like a practice schedule. The first practice was this afternoon. "THANK YOU? BUT DON'T YOU HAVE TO TRY OUT FOR BASKETBALL? ISN'T THEIR SEASON, LIKE, NEARLY OVER? AND I HAVE PLANS THIS AFTERNOON, WITH MY GIRLFRIEND."

That's when I remembered, the basketball team was actually doing really well this season. According to the morning announcements, they were only two games away from being regional champions, and then they would go to the state championships.

Great, I thought. *So Joe and I will be diving right into the fire.*

Gerther shook his head dismissively. "NORMALLY

YOU WOULD HAVE TO TRY OUT, BUT I'VE MADE AN ARRANGEMENT WITH COACH PEROTTA," he said. "YOU BOYS JUST SHOW UP AT PRACTICE TODAY. I'M SORRY, JOE, BUT YOU CAN SEE YOUR GIRLFRIEND SOME OTHER TIME. I KNOW, JOE, THAT YOU'RE A TALENTED ATHLETE. AND FRANK . . ." He paused and turned to look at me. "I'M SURE YOU WILL CATCH ON."

Yup, greeeeeeeat.

"WHAT ABOUT THE B-SHARPS?" I demanded. *What about my dream?* I thought.

Principal Gerther shrugged. "IF YOU CAN HANDLE BOTH, FINE," he said. "BUT IF NOT, BASKETBALL COMES FIRST. I INSIST."

I pulled my mouth into a tight line, biting back any argument. I knew Principal Gerther. I knew he wasn't going to change his mind. Joe shot me a sympathetic look.

Principal Gerther settled back in his chair. "IF WE UNDERSTAND ONE ANOTHER," he said, "YOU BOYS CAN LEAVE. I BELIEVE IT'S YOUR LUNCHTIME. GO ON AND HEAD TO THE CAFETERIA."

I looked behind us at the clock over the doorway. Gerther was right—the assembly would have ended five minutes earlier. My chance at stardom had been dashed. I would have to bury my disappointment in a turkey sandwich.

"AH, OKAY," said Joe, standing slowly, like he expected Gerther to explain more at any moment. "THANK YOU?"

"YOU'RE WELCOME," barked Principal Gerther, gathering up the loose files on his desk. It was clear the meeting was over.

"This is just freakin' weird," Joe muttered, poking his plastic fork into a row of peas. "I'm really sorry, Marianne."

Joe's girlfriend of two weeks, Marianne Sugarman, shrugged and took a sip of coconut water. Marianne was New Agey and a little ethereal, and I honestly had no idea what she and Joe had in common. She was nice, though.

"It's okay," she said in her melodic voice. "I wish we could hang out, but I get it. It's not like you can say no to Principal Gerther."

"I just don't get why he needs us to play *basketball*," Joe muttered, suddenly squishing the pile of peas under the flat side of his fork.

I knew he was upset then. Joe is protective of his peas.

"Maybe it's just what he said," Marianne suggested with a shrug. "He's worried about your transcripts and wants you to have a better shot with colleges. That's nice of him, right?"

Joe shot me a look that said, *There is no way Principal Gerther would do something nice for us, and we both know it.*

"There has to be *some* reason behind it," I said mildly. "And I guess we'll find out soon enough."

OUT OF BOUNDS

2

JOE

H, THE SMELL OF A SCHOOL GYM. The sweat, the tears, the forgotten lunch that's been moldering away in the locker room for a week.

When Frank and I arrived at the gym promptly after the end of school, a bunch of guys were already there wearing their gym clothes and practicing layups. I felt their curious eyes on my brother and me as we headed for the coach's office.

A light-haired, preppy-looking guy wearing a hoodie sat at the desk inside.

"Hi," I greeted him.

He looked up with no recognition. "Hello," he said a bit warily. "I'm Assistant Coach Noonan. Can I help you?"

"Um, we hope so," Frank said. "We're Frank and Joe Hardy? We were told to come to the varsity team practice today. We're joining the team."

Coach Noonan let out a tense little laugh. "Uh, you're *joining* the team?" he asked. "I'm afraid there's been some mistake. First of all, you have to *try out* to join the team. Secondly, the season is nearly over. Even if we were open to new members, you couldn't join now."

I glanced at Frank. *Cool, can we leave then?*

"That's what *we* thought," Frank said with a friendly smile, "but Principal Gerther told us . . ."

Suddenly I heard footsteps behind me and then a taller, dark-haired guy wearing a baseball cap walked up. He had a BHS athletic jacket on and was twirling a whistle that hung around his neck. "Aha," he said, looking at me and Frank with recognition, but no warmth. "Are you Frank and Joe Hardy?"

"That's us," I said.

Coach Noonan stood and came out from behind the desk. "Rich, is there something I should know?" he asked.

Coach Perotta shook his head, and I caught a little blink-and-you'd-miss-it eye roll. "Joe and Frank are joining the team for the rest of the season, Bob. I've spoken to Principal Gerther about it and will explain it all later."

Coach Noonan's face got all pinchy. "Rich, we have regional championships this Friday," he said in a tight voice. "Do you think it's a good idea to introduce two new—"

"We'll talk about it later," Coach Perotta said smoothly. I caught Frank's eye: *The coaches don't want us here either. What's going on?* "Anyway, boys, did you bring anything else to wear?" He eyed our jeans, Frank's button-down, and my thick sweater.

We shook our heads. "We didn't exactly know we were coming here this morning," Frank explained.

Coach Perotta let out a tiny sigh. "All right," he said. "Let's get you guys some gym clothes, and then we can get started. I have a feeling you are going to need a lot of practice to get up to speed."

"YOU NEED TO STAY ON THE BALL!" Coach Perotta screamed at my brother about an hour and a half later. Frank was sweaty and red-faced, doing his best, but his slow, high dribble was easily stolen by a kid named Dorian, who made a score. "Try it again. AGAIN!"

Dorian retrieved the ball and threw it back to Frank—a little too hard, in my opinion. "Sorry," he said with a toothy smile that implied he wasn't sorry at all.

"Dude!" A kid whose name I didn't know yet shoved me forward, as another kid thrust the ball into my hands. I was in a line practicing three-point throws, across the gym from Frank. "It's your turn! You need to pay attention!"

Right! I tried to line up the ball just right, but I could hear the other guys grumbling to themselves behind me. *I'm taking too long.* They worked like a well-oiled machine: catch, aim, throw. Catch, aim, throw. I threw the ball, but all the tension had thrown me off and it sailed off to the left, not even hitting the backboard.

"Jeez!" yelled the kid behind me. Charlie, I think. "How did you guys get on this team?"

I tried to ignore it and just walked to the back of the line, taking the opportunity to look over at Frank. He was trying to dribble lower but he was clearly exhausted; the ball darted away from him, bouncing out of bounds. I could hear the jeers and taunts from across the gym.

Basketball is hard. That seemed to be the underlying message here. It wasn't the kind of skill you could learn in two hours, and it was clear that neither the coaches nor the players were willing to make any allowances for us being new. I was faring a little better than Frank, but not by much. It was *very* clear that neither one of us was ready to win any championships.

TWEET! A whistle trilled through the gym, and I turned around to see Coach Perotta raising his hand. "All right, guys, enough drills for today. Let's have a quick meeting."

I followed the other guys as they gathered in the center of the gym, sitting on the circle that surrounded the Bayport Tiger, our mascot.

Coach Perotta cleared his throat. "It's clear that we have a lot of work to do here," he said, not even bothering to hide the fact that he was staring straight at Frank and me. "Wouldn't you agree, Coach Noonan?"

"Definitely," said the assistant coach. His eyes looked slightly warmer than Perotta's, though. "It's going to take a lot of practice . . . but we need to stay positive."

"Stay positive?" a worried voice piped up from the other side of the circle. I looked over: *Dorian*. "Can we be real for a minute? *Why* are these two guys joining the team right now? They weren't even on junior varsity."

Coach Perotta cleared his throat. "Dorian, I've told you, it's complicated, but it's not up for debate. Frank and Joe are part of the team now."

"They're going to bring us down," another voice insisted, closer to me. I turned and saw a kid whose name I didn't know, but who was in the three-point drill with me. "They're going to cost us the state championship. It isn't fair!"

Other voices piped up in agreement, and soon the whole circle was chiming in with "That's right" and "It's not fair" and "Who are these guys, even?"

Coach Perotta looked like he was trying to figure out what to say. It wasn't hard to tell from his manner that he agreed with a lot of what the guys were saying. But for whatever reason, Principal Gerther had told him we had to join the team. Why?

It wasn't Coach Perotta who spoke next, but a guy sitting a few seats away from Frank.

"Guys, just chill," he said. "You're being ugly to these guys. They really tried today. And if they're on the team for sure now, then it's on us to help them get better, not make it harder for them."

His name was Jason Bound. I knew because he was all over the morning announcements and the school newspaper. He was the team captain, star of the basketball team, and he had already secured a scholarship to Duke next year.

He'd seemed nice enough during practice, but his words still surprised me. I realized when he spoke that I'd sort of been agreeing with all the complaints. What *were* Frank and I doing here? Was it really fair to saddle this championship-bound team with two novice players who hadn't even tried out?

Jason's words reminded me that none of us really had a choice in the matter. We'd better make the best of it.

Coach Perotta looked at him gratefully. "Thank you, Jason. You make a good point—we're all in this together. Frank and Joe are on the team now, and that means we need to support them."

Not long after that, Coach Perotta sent us back to the locker room to shower and change. None of the players said anything to us, but the grumbling and dirty looks seemed to have ceased for now. Frank and I showered and put our school clothes back on. By the time we were ready to go, most of the team had already left.

We walked in silence out of the gym and toward the student parking lot. Finally Frank said, "I think I'm going to be pretty sore tomorrow."

"Yeah," I agreed. "That was really hard."

"What do you think Principal Gerther's deal is?" Frank asked. "Does he *not* want the team to be state champions? Because it seems like a championship would look good for both him and the school, right?"

"And it seems like if he just didn't want them to win," I said, "there are easier ways—"

"Hey, guys!"

I jumped a bit. I'd been so busy talking to Frank I hadn't noticed Jason walking through the parking lot toward us.

"Oh! Uh . . . hey, Jason." I smiled. "Thanks for saying what you did back there. It was really nice of you."

Jason shrugged. "It's no big thing. I meant what I said. We're a team, and if you're part of the team now, then we should support you."

"Thanks." Frank nodded at him. "It's great to get that kind of support from the team captain."

Jason grinned. "Honestly, I was impressed by how you took everything back there. That was *not* an easy practice. Most people would have just given up and walked out the door. But you stuck with it. That says something about your character, I think. We can use guys like you on the team."

I glanced at Frank. Jason's speech inside had impressed me, but this was even more surprising. Jason was the team captain and star player—he arguably had the most riding on the team's success this year. And yet he was going out of his way to be nice to us.

"Thanks, man," said Frank with a smile. "That means a lot, coming from you."

"Tell you what," Jason said. "I know the guys weren't super cool to you back there, but maybe they just need to get to know you better. One of our players, Steve, has a birthday tonight. We're meeting up at Paco's Pizza to celebrate. Six thirty. Want to come?"

I looked at Frank. I had a ton of homework, and after practice, we wouldn't get home till five. But an opportunity to bond with our teammates seemed too good to pass up.

"We'll be there," said my brother.

"Great!" Jason flashed a huge smile at us. "See you then."

He walked off in the direction of his car, and Frank and I headed to ours.

"Getting to know our teammates better can't be a bad thing," I said.

"Yep," Frank agreed, unlocking the doors. "And maybe it will bring us a little closer to figuring out why we're on the team in the first place."

A couple of hours later, we pulled into the parking lot of Paco's Pizza. The shack-like restaurant was on the very edge of town, bordering an industrial area. We'd had to look it up on Google Maps, since we'd never heard of the place before.

"Why here?" Frank asked, looking around at the near-empty parking lot. "Everyone knows Pizza Palace has the best pizza in town."

"That's *your* opinion," I reminded him. "You'll recall that my heart belongs to Luigi's."

"This just seems kind of . . . off the beaten path," Frank mused, still staring.

He turned off the ignition. "Let's go in," I said, unclipping my seat belt. "Maybe this place has the best Sicilian slice in town, and we just don't know it yet."

"Color me dubious," Frank replied, but he got out of the car anyway.

It was late winter, and still getting dark around six. There were few lights in the parking lot, but the inside of the restaurant was illuminated with warm yellow light.

"There's no one in there," Frank pointed out.

I angled my head and tried to get a good look. "Are you sure?" I asked. "We can't see the back."

"There's only one other car in the parking lot," Frank said. "That's probably whoever's working. The place is empty."

I glanced at my watch. "We're, like, two minutes early," I said. "You know how people are. Let's just go in there and—"

That was when someone grabbed me from behind and shoved something over my head, and everything went black.

MASKED ENEMIES

3

FRANK

ONCE THE BAGS WERE OVER OUR heads, someone swiftly pulled my wrists behind my back and bound them with what felt like duct tape. Then whoever it was grabbed both of us up off our feet—there were clearly a bunch of them—and carried us far enough that we must have left the parking lot. I heard a car door opening, and then the *creeeeeeak* of a trunk lid. Then we were dumped inside the tight, cramped trunk, shoved into the fetal position. They bound our ankles in the same way as our wrists. The trunk lid shut heavily on top of us, and a minute or so later, the engine started and we were moving.

"What the . . . ?" Joe's voice came out muffled, but I could understand him. Luckily, they hadn't gagged us.

What the . . . ? indeed. Whoever these guys were, they weren't the first to throw a bag over my head and dump me in a trunk, and they probably wouldn't be the last. Those are just the wages of being an amateur detective in a town filled with unoriginal crooks.

"Do you think Gerther is trying to kill us?" Joe asked.

"Doubtful," I replied. "There are easier ways to do it. And that wouldn't explain the whole joining-the-basketball-team thing."

"So did Jason Bound set us up?" Joe asked.

"Obviously," I replied. "He told us to go to Paco's, right? Did you see anyone else there?"

"No."

"So the birthday story was a setup. The only question is . . . why? What are they going to do to us?"

"I have a feeling we're about to find out," Joe mumbled.

We drove around for what seemed like about twenty minutes. At first I closed my eyes and tried to keep track of the direction, so I'd have a rough idea where they were taking us. But soon I gave up. It's too hard to estimate distance with a bag over your head inside a locked trunk.

Finally the car pulled to a stop, and a few seconds later the trunk popped open. I could feel the cold outside air blowing in.

Nobody said anything as we were hauled out, our restraints were cut, and we were placed upright on our feet. What must have been two people flanked me on either side, each grabbing an elbow and guiding me to walk alongside them on a hard surface, probably a driveway. I heard a door open and then was guided inside, someone's hand on my head warning me to duck.

We walked down a narrow flight of stairs. Then I was guided a few more feet and stopped. One of the people shepherding me poked my shin and then guided my foot up off the ground, onto what felt like a little pedestal or something in front of me. Then I was pushed to step up onto the little pedestal, which I realized was *quite* small, maybe the size of the narrow end of a cinder block. I could hear the sounds of others helping Joe do the same a few feet away. The guiders held me up until I was able to balance on my own—and then suddenly they were gone.

I wobbled on the little pedestal, whatever it was, wondering what was going on. Was it safe? I was up high enough that I felt like I could get hurt if I fell suddenly.

"What is this?" I yelled, trying to keep the panic out of my voice. "What do you want?"

"What do you think we want?"

The voice that came back was freaky—deep and distorted, clearly coming from a voice modulator.

"I—well—"

Before I could get an answer out, the bag was suddenly ripped off my head.

I sucked in a breath.

Joe and I were standing in a dark room with no

windows—likely a basement, I figured. But someone had switched on a black light. And in front of us, standing in a row, were five people in long black robes, wearing weird masks that hid their faces. The masks had been painted with bold white designs that caught the black light in a seriously creepy way.

I glanced over at Joe, who was staring, openmouthed, at the figures in the masks.

Then I looked down at my feet. Joe and I had both been placed on pedestals about eighteen inches high. As I'd assumed, each pedestal was the size and thickness of a cinder block, but they had us standing on the narrow end. Mine wobbled ominously as I struggled to keep my balance.

As I went to put down my foot, I was startled by the loudest buzzing sound I'd ever heard. Both Joe and I were so stunned we fell off the pedestals. I managed to catch myself with my foot, but Joe landed in a heap.

"*That's strike one*," the bizarre voice intoned. "*Brothers, hand down the punishment.*"

One of the masked figures stepped forward, holding a mug. He walked behind me, pulled down the back of my shirt, and poured the contents of the mug down my back.

"*Auuugh!*" The mug was full of hot water. Not hot enough to cause serious burn damage, but hot enough to hurt—especially when coupled with surprise. The water soaked the back of my shirt so that it stuck to my skin.

The figure walked over to Joe and did the same, pouring more water down *his* back. Joe yelped.

"That water is one hundred and sixty degrees. Each time you fall off the pedestal, the water will get hotter, all the way up to boiling point. Make your choices accordingly. Brothers, help them back onto the pedestals."

I looked at Joe, sending him a silent thought. *This is not good.* Whatever these guys were up to, they were obviously willing to hurt us. And I had no idea who they were, which meant they could do so without consequences.

Two masked people came over and got me back up on the pedestal, and others did the same for Joe. When I was back up, I tried to focus on my balance and stay upright. It wasn't easy. It took constant focus; my legs began shaking after just a few seconds.

After a brief silence, the lead figure spoke again: *"Frank and Joe Hardy, you have destroyed the sanctity of our brotherhood by joining us uninvited and unwanted. For this, you deserve to be punished. We've brought you here tonight to get answers. Are you willing to give them?"*

"That depends," I said honestly.

"*Brothers*," said the lead figure.

Without further ado, one of the figures on the right stepped forward, reached up, and punched me in the kidneys. This caused me to swoon and nearly fall off the pedestal—but I managed to catch myself just in time.

"That is the wrong answer. Let's see if you can follow along.

It's clear that Coach Perotta was told that you would join the team—this wasn't his idea. So whose was it?"

This time I was silent. I glanced at Joe, whose mouth remained shut. He looked resolute.

"*Brothers*," said the lead figure.

This time two of them came forward. The one on the right wound up and punched me in the stomach, causing me to double over, while the one on the left walked up to Joe and punched him in the kidneys. He moaned.

"Why do you want to know?" I managed to squeeze out through the pain. "What difference does it make?"

"*It matters very much*," the lead figure said. "*Our brotherhood has much at stake in the next few weeks. We need to know who our enemies are.*"

Brotherhood? Much at stake? We had to be talking about the basketball team, right? But why were they acting like they were some kind of secret fraternity instead of just a school-sponsored sports team?

"Why do you assume it's an enemy?" Joe asked. "Maybe we were sent to help."

The lead figure threw back his head and laughed—still distorted by the voice modulator. "*That's very funny. Clearly you didn't see yourselves play today.*"

He paused, and neither Joe nor I spoke. There was silence for a minute.

"*Very well*," said the lead figure, breaking the silence. "*Clearly more motivation is needed. You are convinced that you belong among us. Brothers, bring forward the brand."*

A figure on the left reached inside his robe and pulled out a small, shiny object. He held it up.

"*This is a team pin*," the lead figure said, "*with the logo for the Bayport Tigers. If we heat this over a candle until it's red-hot, we can use it to brand you both.*"

I involuntarily jumped. "*Brand* us?"

"That's right. If you are so determined to be part of the team, surely you are willing to wear our brand on your skin? It will burn for a moment, yes, but then it will mark you as one of us forever."

"Wait . . . , " said Joe, unable to hide the fear in his voice. "do you . . . *brand* all the players? Is that a thing?"

The lead figure cackled again. *"Whether we do or not, no one will ever tell. But being a true brother doesn't come without cost. If you really wish to avoid this fate, you can tell us right now who sent you."*

Joe and I traded glances. The look on his face said, *Holy frijoles, but I don't think we should tell them, right?* And I tried to make my expression say, *Yeah, and they can't really* brand *us. They'd get in so much trouble! Right? Right?!*

"*Very well*," the lead figure intoned. The brother who'd held up the pin took out a lighter and a pair of tongs. He handed the lighter to the guy next to him, who coaxed out a flame, and then placed the pin in the pincers of the tongs and held it right in the middle of the flame.

I could smell something burning. The metal began to glow.

Joe made a squeaky noise. I glanced at him: *Be cool.*

Then the lighter clicked off and the brother holding the pin with the tongs turned to look at us. He began to walk toward Joe, holding out the pin. . . .

I felt my heart speed up and began to sweat. *They wouldn't, would they? Surely . . .*

"Pull up his sleeve!" the leader intoned.

Joe let out a sound like he was being strangled.

"IT WAS PRINCIPAL GERTHER!"

The words came out of my mouth without my ever planning to say them. But when they did, everyone turned to me, and the brother holding the pin lowered it. Joe swayed and nearly fell off his pedestal, but was able to balance at the last minute.

"What was that?" asked the lead figure.

I tried to breathe. "It was Principal Gerther," I said in a rush. "He called us into his office and said we had to join the team."

"Why?" asked the lead figure. He'd forgotten to use the voice modulator this time, so I tried to memorize the sound of his voice. It was familiar, but not obviously so—I couldn't immediately place it with any of the players I'd met that day.

"We don't know," Joe said. "Your guess is as good as ours, really. We've been trying to figure it out all day."

The lead figure looked at the masked figures around him. I sensed he was trying to decide whether to believe us.

"Why would he tell you to join the team and not tell you why?"

Joe and I both shrugged.

"Why does he wear the same polyester suit every day?"

Joe asked. "Why did he pull Frank out of an extracurricular activity to tell him he has no extracurricular activities? Why *anything?* I can't explain Principal Gerther to you."

The lead figure dropped the voice modulator and turned to the others. There was some hushed whispering as they seemed to discuss whether to accept that or not. The brief break in the action gave me the chance to remember that balancing on this block was making my legs ache like heck. My weak muscles from that day's practice weren't helping either.

I glanced at Joe. My expression: *Do you think they'll let us go?* His expression: *Who can predict anything in this crazy world?*

Finally the discussion seemed to break up, and the masked figures turned to face us again. The lead figure spoke.

"We have chosen to believe you truly don't know Principal Gerther's motivation. But the fact remains: you do not belong in the brotherhood. The brotherhood has bonded and suffered together. We deserve to be there, but you two do not.

"This is what will happen: tomorrow the two of you will go to Principal Gerther's office and announce you're quitting the team. No explanation. You will take whatever punishment he hands down. And after that, you can go about your lives as normal. If you never speak of this again, we have no reason to seek revenge."

Here the masked figure paused and cleared his throat. When he spoke again, even with the modulator, I could tell that the tone was lower and more serious.

"If you don't, you boys will regret that you were ever born.

You have not yet seen what the brotherhood is capable of. Our reach extends far beyond this room, or this town, even. If you boys want a future, you will quit."

I glanced at Joe. Both of our expressions: *Daaaaaaaaaaang.*

"*Do you understand?*"

"I understand," I said. *I understand that I want to get off this darn pedestal.*

The figure turned to Joe. *"I need both of you to say it."*

Joe nodded. "I understand," he said.

"Very well. Brothers?"

Faster than I would have thought possible, the masked figures advanced on us. I was dragged down from the pedestal, the bag thrown back over my head, my hands bound with what felt like tape. We were led back up the stairs, out onto the driveway, and back into the trunk, and then our ankles were bound. The trunk lid slammed down on us, and the engine started up again.

We were bouncing along for a minute or two when Joe muttered, "Well, that wasn't fun."

"Yeah," I agreed. "Not what I expected at all."

"Did I almost get *branded*?" Joe asked.

"I'm not sure," I admitted. "Do you think they really would have done it?"

"It sure felt like it," Joe said.

"What do we do now?" I asked.

Joe groaned. "Get home," he said. "Have some of Aunt Trudy's leftovers. Then decide."

After a few minutes the engine stopped. Seconds later the car doors opened and the trunk was popped. Cool air flooded in as hands reached down to lift us out and carry us . . . somewhere.

Suddenly I was placed in a semi-upright position on something cold and metal, sitting down. I could hear Joe being positioned nearby.

Then there was a scurrying sound, doors opening and slamming, and a car driving away.

"Did they seriously just leave us here tied up?" Joe asked.

"I think so," I said.

Joe groaned and I could hear him begin to struggle. "It's, like, thirty degrees out here. Do you think you can wiggle out of your restraints?"

I tried, but they were too tight. "Negative. We're going to have to wait here for someone to find us."

"Where do you think we are?"

I sighed. "Hopefully in front of a Walmart or something. Somewhere really busy."

But that seemed doubtful. Once the car drove away, we didn't hear another one for a few minutes. It sounded like we were on an out-of-the-way street.

It felt like six hours, but was probably only thirty minutes or so, before we heard the rumble of a car approaching, then a door opening and shutting, followed by a startled, "What the . . . ?" from a young-sounding male voice.

I heard footsteps approaching, and the bag was ripped

off my head. I was looking at a startled, pimply-faced teenager in a Paco's polo shirt and baseball cap. We were back in Paco's parking lot, propped in the small outdoor seating area, and on the ground by my feet were four large pizza boxes. The kid turned and ripped off Joe's bag.

"Seriously?" he said, as he pulled out a pocketknife and sliced the duct tape around our wrists and ankles. "This is, like, the third time this month! Don't you guys have anything better to do than play stupid practical jokes on one another?"

I looked at Joe. "We most certainly do. Thanks for the rescue."

We walked over to our car, which was thankfully still parked where we'd left it at 6:28. That felt like days ago, but when Joe turned on the car, the digital clock read 8:24.

We looked at each other. "Let's get home," I said. "It's been a *very* long day."

GAME ON 4

JOE

H, HEY THERE, *JASON*, FANCY MEETING you here!" I said, sliding a book titled *Trial by Fire: Hazing and You* across the circulation desk to our friendly school library volunteer. I'd chosen the book as a not-so-subtle signal, because it was clear to us after what happened last night that the basketball team had a problem with hazing: harassing or ridiculing certain members to make them do what team members wanted. College fraternities and sororities are notorious for hazing, but it happens sometimes on sports teams too. Since the basketball team was school-sponsored, hazing was *definitely* against the rules and could get whoever was doing it in serious trouble. The question was, who was doing it?

Jason Bound looked up with a nonplussed expression. He

glanced from me to Frank, who stood just behind me. We'd used our sleuthing capabilities (and Marianne's role as first-period office aide) to deduce that Jason helped out in the library during our lunch break.

We figured it was the safest place to ask him *what the heck??* Surely he wouldn't want to make a scene in such a quiet place, with a bunch of students and the real librarian around.

He scanned the book's bar code and sneered at us. "Fancy meeting *you two* here," he said. "Student ID?"

I handed mine over, and he scanned it. I'd just been trying to make a point with the book, but it looked like I was checking it out now.

Jason pushed the book at me, looking up at us with an unimpressed expression. "Did you two have fun last night?"

I glared at him. I couldn't believe he was being so open about this. "Of course we didn't."

Jason shrugged. "Well, maybe next time you'll take my invitation seriously."

"We took everything you said seriously," Frank said, eyebrows raised with meaning. "Though it's a lot easier to see your face now."

Jason looked at Frank like he'd lost his mind. "You couldn't see my face in the parking lot?" he asked.

"Uh, *no*," I said, surprised that he'd admitted it so quickly. "There was the small matter of the bag on my head."

"What are you talking about?" Jason asked. "You had a bag on your head in the school parking lot yesterday?"

I glanced at Frank, confused, then turned back to Jason. "What are *you* talking about?" I asked.

Jason frowned now. "I'm talking about when I made a point to track you down yesterday and invite you to meet us for pizza," he said very slowly, like he was talking to a small child. "Then you never showed up."

I stared at him. "Wait, you mean . . . you guys really went to Paco's?"

Jason glared at me. "*Of course* we did," he said. "Did you think it was tentative or something? Did you get a better offer?"

"No, we showed up!" Frank said defensively.

Jason scowled at him. "When?" he demanded. "I was there the whole time, and we were *right* by the door. It's not that big of a place."

"How long were you there?" I asked.

Jason shrugged. "A couple hours. We had a good time." He sighed and began typing something into the computer. "You know, I wanted to be nice to you guys, because you seemed like cool people. But standing people up is just rude."

"Um . . . ," Frank started, holding up a hand. "Jason, do you *really* not know what happened to us last night?"

Jason stopped typing and looked at us, his eyes widening with concern. "What, were you in an accident or something?" he asked. "Because you could have just said so. Is there something I *should* know?"

I looked at Frank. If Jason was putting on an act, he was a *really* good actor.

"No," I said quickly, picking up the book. "Look, I'm really sorry we didn't make it. See you at practice later?"

Jason met my eyes, clearly more confused than ever. If he was mad that we were still planning to go to practice, there was no hint of it in his expression. "Okay," he said. "See you then, I guess."

I nodded at Frank and led him out of the library, dropping the hazing book in the "return" box along the way.

"What the heck?" I asked once we were back in the hall. "I didn't necessarily expect him to come out and admit it, but that was *really* good acting, if he was part of what happened last night."

"I know," Frank said. "I thought that would go differently."

I sighed. "What now?" I asked. "Should we go to Gerther?"

We'd stayed up late the night before figuring out a plan of action. We finally decided to start with Jason—since he was most likely to be involved in the scheme. It was clear that whoever was behind this expected us to quit, but we weren't sure we were ready. We knew we'd be putting ourselves at risk until we left the team. But we wanted to find out as much as we could in the meantime.

Frank frowned. "I don't *want* to now," he said, shaking his head.

"But we said we would!" I pointed out. "They're going to come after us again if we don't, Frank. And who *knows* what they'll try next? They tried to *brand* me."

Frank sighed. "We don't know that they would have gone through with it."

"Well, awesome," I retorted, getting frustrated myself. "Do you want to take that bet? It's only *my arm.*"

Frank shook his head. "No, I don't. But listen, Joe: these guys are bullies, plain and simple. If we quit, then they get what they want, and they get to keep doing this to other people. Remember what the pizza guy said."

"Third time this month," I said.

"That means they make a habit of this," Frank replied. "It isn't right. We've never given in to bullies before, and I don't think we should now."

It was my turn to sigh. "We don't know what they're capable of, Frank," I said. "Or even who they are. If they get us again, they can do whatever they want, and we can't finger them for it."

"I know," Frank said with a serious expression. "But we're in the business of solving problems, and there's clearly a big hazing problem on the basketball team. Deep down, you must realize this is why Gerther had us join in the first place."

I groaned. Truthfully, the thought had crossed my mind.

"I think we have a moral obligation to get to the bottom of it," Frank said. "Or at least to find out more."

I looked at him skeptically, but he just gazed back, totally sincere. I groaned again; I wanted to punch something. Not my brother, because I was pretty sure he was right.

"All right," I said, grudgingly. "But I just hope we hold on to all our critical body parts in the process."

There was an away basketball game that afternoon, and to say that Frank and I were ready for it after only one day of practice would be . . . a lie, actually. Our only hope was that the coaches would decide to have us watch the entire game from the safety of the sidelines. We also wondered what our teammates' reactions would be to our presence—if some among them had been involved in the hazing, they'd realize that we weren't quitting the team.

When we boarded the bus after school, I studied each teammate's face carefully to see who looked surprised or dismayed. Whoever the masked hazers were, they weren't expecting to see us show up on the bus, and they surely wouldn't be happy about it. But as I scanned their faces, I felt halfway disappointed and halfway impressed. Nobody's face betrayed anything. The girls' team was on the bus as well—their game was right before ours—so a lot of the guys were chatting up the girls. Whoever the hazers were, they were pros.

I grabbed Frank's arm. "Let's split up," I whispered. "If we strike up conversations with our seatmates, maybe we'll learn if anything similar has happened to other people."

He slipped into a seat next to a junior named Ty. I kept walking and finally slid into a bench next to a sophomore, Gabe. I'd noticed at practice yesterday that he was small, but really fast.

"Hey," I said, trying to look friendly. "I'm Joe."

He nodded, pulling out headphones. "Gabe," he said. "Whassup?"

Friendly, I noted. *Either doesn't hate me or is good at faking it.*

"Not much," I said. "Kind of nervous about this game, honestly."

The bus rumbled to a start and we began driving toward Mill Valley, where the game would be played.

"The first game is tough," Gabe said knowingly. "You just have to play your best."

"When was your first game?" I asked.

"This past fall," he replied with a shrug. "It was tough. But at least I had a bunch of other guys starting with me."

"How many guys on the team were new last fall?" I asked.

Gabe thought a minute. "Maybe ten, twelve?"

"Was it . . . hard?" I asked. "I mean, the team seems pretty tight. And I've heard . . ." I paused, looked around, and lowered my voice. No one near us seemed to be listening. "Rumors."

Gabe looked startled. "Um . . . what do you mean?"

I cleared my throat. "I've heard if you don't play well, things might happen to you."

Gabe suddenly seemed uncomfortable. *Jackpot,* I thought. "Oh, that's probably exaggerated," he said. "I wouldn't worry."

Time to go in for the kill. "Did that happen to you?" I whispered.

"What?" he asked nervously.

I looked around again to make sure no one was listening, then leaned in. "Did something . . . *happen*, if you didn't play well?"

Gabe's eyes darted around anxiously.

I lowered my voice even further. "I just want to be prepared, if anything goes down. I know I didn't play so great yesterday. I want to try my best, but . . ." I paused. "I also want to know what's in store for me."

Gabe seemed really nervous now. He looked from me, to his hands clenched in his lap.

"Can I tell you something?" I whispered. "Something happened last night. . . ." In the lowest voice I could manage, I gave him a play-by-play of the night before—including the pedestal and the near branding. At certain points Gabe's eyes widened in what looked like recognition.

"I'm just not sure how much more I can take," I said finally. I was being sincere, too. "Can you tell me what happens if you don't do what they want?"

By this point Gabe had flushed bright red. He looked all around him, like he wanted to see whether anyone was listening. Seemingly satisfied, he leaned in and said in a very quiet voice, "Well—"

"HEY, GABE, ARE YOU WEARING A BIEBER T-SHIRT IRONICALLY, OR WHAT?"

Gabe and I both jumped about a foot in the air at the sound of a loud female voice sliding into the bench behind us.

The girl was Kelly Pritzky. I knew from the school blog that she was captain of the girls' basketball team, which was having a pretty good season too, although their successes were being overshadowed by Jason Bound and the boys' possible championship. She was tall, freckled, red-haired, and loud. I think she'd been voted "Class Cutup" in the senior awards.

Now she looked at Gabe's T-shirt as he turned around, shell-shocked. "Oh, my bad. That's just, like, a graphic thing. It looks *totally* like this Justin Bieber T-shirt my little cousin's been wearing around. I just want to say to her parents, are you *serious* with this? I mean, really?"

Not sure exactly what to do, I went with a formal introduction. "Hi," I said, holding out my hand to shake. "I'm Joe Hardy."

She shook my hand, not seeming fazed by my formality. "Whassup. Kelly Pritzky. You're one of the new guys, right?"

I nodded. "Yeah, that's me."

She narrowed her eyes. "I'd ask you what the heck you're doing joining the team right now, but I gather that's confidential information."

I swallowed hard. *Confidential information?* Had she heard about the hazing last night, the failed attempt to get us to spill?

She shrugged, breaking the tension. "Anyway, I don't care. Jason says you're decent guys, and he's a good judge of character. Are you nervous about today's game?"

We started making small talk, me going on about how

hard the practice was, Kelly laughing and sharing memories of her first few weeks on the team. I liked her, actually. She was really brash and honest and funny.

I just wished she hadn't interrupted Gabe in the middle of his opening up to me.

Eventually our conversation wrapped up, and Kelly left to go chat with her teammates. By that time the kid in front of us had struck up a conversation with Gabe, though, and it seemed like my opportunity to get any information out of him had passed.

After about an hour, we pulled up in front of Mill Valley's very modern high school. The driver opened the doors, and Coach Noonan yelled for us to get off.

I ended up next to Frank once we'd filed off the bus. "Find out anything interesting?" I asked.

He frowned. "Kind of? I got sucked into this conversation about *The Walking Dead*, so I know a lot about zombies now. Did I learn anything about the case? No. You?"

I shook my head. But just at that moment, Gabe scooted past me, quickly reaching out for my hand and pressing a small piece of paper into it. I grabbed it, and he headed past me into the gym without even making eye contact.

I grabbed Frank's elbow and pulled him to the outskirts of the crowd, where I unfolded the note and showed it to him.

I CAN'T TALK NOW. E-MAIL ME:
GABEZ@FASTMAIL.COM

HACK ATTACK 5

FRANK

THE GAME WAS A REAL NAIL-BITER. Nonstop action, with lots of interceptions, complicated plays, three-point throws. . . . I mean, you had to be a pretty amazing athlete to hold your own in this game.

Which is why Joe and I spent the entire game on the bench. Okay, not the entire game. When Jayden Speck fell and twisted his ankle, Joe was put in for, like, forty-five seconds. Then he missed an easy pass, and Jayden told Coach Perotta through gritted teeth, "I feel better." Soon Joe was riding the pine again and Jayden hobbled back into the action.

That was Joe, though, not me. For the entire game, my backside might as well have been Krazy-glued to the bench.

At one point I caught Coach Noonan watching me with

sympathy. "You'll play soon," he mouthed. But the truth was, *not* playing was kind of a relief. It gave me no chance to mess up, to make the team members who didn't want me there even angrier.

And it gave me the opportunity to watch and listen.

Jason Bound was really an amazing player. There were other good athletes on the team, but Jason was in another league entirely. Dorian Marte seemed to be his second-in-command, setting him up for layups and stuff like that. He was fast and strong too, but nowhere near as good as Jason. Dorian was only a junior, though, so I figured he would be the star of the team next year.

You could tell that the whole team had been practicing together for a long time, though. They had a chemistry that only comes with months and months of work. Watching them play, I could understand how a lot of the team members weren't happy we'd just shown up at practice one day. There *wasn't* time to get us up to speed with the rest of the team. We were just going to hold them back.

Near the end of the game, another junior named Steve O'Brien was called out and settled on the bench next to me. For a few minutes he was totally silent, watching the game intently, so I didn't try to make conversation. But after two or three minutes he suddenly turned to me and asked, "So why didn't you guys show up last night?"

"Sorry?" I asked, startled. I'd been watching Dorian intercept one of Mill Valley's strongest players.

"DEFENSE!" the Mill Valley coach was yelling.

"At Paco's," Steve said, looking at me with genuine disappointment. "We were there to celebrate my birthday. Jason said he'd invited you and Joe."

I stared at Steve. Was he being serious right now? Did that mean he *wasn't* involved with the weird masked guys, or maybe didn't even know that was happening?

Or was he playing a part now? If so, he was doing a great job.

Is the hazing problem something just a few team members are involved in? Or is everyone on this team an Academy Award–caliber actor?

"Um, we actually did show up," I said honestly. "But we didn't see anyone inside, so we . . . didn't stay."

"You didn't see anyone inside?" Steve looked confused. "I was there, like, right at seven."

Ahhhh. "Jason told us six thirty," I explained. "That's when we got there."

Recognition dawned in Steve's eyes. "Oh, that blockhead," he muttered, shaking his head. "Jason is the *worst* with time. He should never be left in charge of invitations."

Something was still bothering me, though. "Um, the weird thing is, we did go back," I said, wondering if this would trigger any recognition on Steve's part. "Like, at eight thirtyish? And no one was there then, either."

Steve nodded. "Yeah, we didn't end up staying long," he

said. "We had our pizza, but then Doug mentioned he had the new Call of Duty game. We all went to his house and played for, like, four hours." He chuckled. "My *mom* ended up calling me, dude. We totally lost track of time."

I frowned, still stuck on his first point. "What time did you leave?" I asked. "Jason said you were there for two hours, at least."

Steve groaned and shook his head. "See my previous comment about Jason and time," he said. "We were there for an hour, maybe. We must've gotten there after you left, and left before you came back. I'm sorry, dude. Next time we get together, *I'll* give you the deets, all right?"

I smiled. "Thanks," I said. "Hey, was Jason there the whole time? I mean, maybe that's why he was totally off on his times."

Steve laughed. "Oh, he was there," he said. "I beat him senseless at Call of Duty. He's just an idiot."

I glanced back up at the game. Jason was, right at that moment, making a three-point shot from the middle of the court. "A talented idiot," I said.

Steve looked at Jason without a trace of jealousy. "You can say that again."

I studied Steve's contented face, wondering if I'd be pushing my luck with another question. "Who else was there?"

He glanced at me, surprised. "Pretty much the whole team? It was a lot of guys."

"Just tell me who you remember," I said.

Steve sighed. "Okay, um, Jason," he said, counting off on his fingers. "Ty, Gabe, Quentin, Juan . . ."

"Was Dorian there?" I asked suddenly. The voice of the masked leader had sounded familiar. And there were only so many voices I'd heard up to that point. Dorian's was one of them.

Steve shook his head. "Dorian never comes out on weeknights," he said. "His mom is, like, super strict."

"Got it," I said, nodding slowly. "Well . . . I'm really sorry we missed it. I hope you had a happy birthday, anyway."

He shrugged. "Pizza and video games. It's the simple things, right?"

"Right." We both turned back to the game. We were up by twelve points. Things were looking good for the Bayport Tigers, and for Jason Bound.

Pizza and video games definitely beats our *night.*

"So you think Jason intentionally gave us the wrong time?" Joe asked as I drove us to school the next morning. I'd told him what I learned from Steve after the game, and we'd been thinking on it ever since.

"It's definitely possible," I said. "He was with them all night, so he couldn't have been one of the masked guys, but that doesn't mean he can't know it's happening. Of all the guys, he has the most to gain if the team stays strong . . . and the most to lose if they don't."

Joe looked thoughtful. "If he has a serious shot at a

basketball career ahead of him, maybe he's trying to keep his hands clean. You know, letting other guys carry out the hazing, in case they get caught, but pulling the strings from a distance."

"Stranger things have happened," I agreed.

Suddenly Joe's phone dinged with an incoming e-mail. He grabbed it from the center console and checked it.

"Want me to read this email from Gabe out loud?" he asked.

"Please," I said.

He read, "'Hey, Joe. Look, I don't want to tell you what to do, but I would *let go* of this. This may seem like a weird little game to you, but these guys are *dangerous*. If you defy them, they will *end* you. I was harassed by those guys for a whole month, but I've been playing better and I'm finally past it. I would never wish what I went through on anyone. There is a rumor that they did something so horrible to Diego Lopez that he quit the team and won't talk about it with anybody. If you guys really want to play basketball, then focus on getting better so they won't target you anymore. If you don't really want to play . . . take their advice and quit. It's not worth it! Don't be a hero. Get out while you can. Gabe.'"

I had pulled into the school parking lot while Joe was reading and now swung the car into a spot. "Wow," Joe said, as I put the car in park and stared out the windshield.

I was quiet for a moment, considering Gabe's words. "Do

you really think they're that dangerous?" I asked. "They're just kids playing games. Aren't they?"

Joe looked at me. "They wanted to *brand me,* bro."

I shook my head. "I still don't think they would have gone through with it."

"For someone who's so sure of that," Joe said, "you told them everything they wanted to know at just the right time."

I frowned. I mean, I couldn't risk it. I still didn't think they would have done it.

Would they?

"Let's think on this," I said after a minute or two. "We can talk about our next steps at lunch. Cool?"

"Cool," Joe agreed, and we got out of the car and headed for our first classes.

For me, this was English with Ms. Kowalski. I'm usually more of a science guy, but I was really enjoying English so far this year. Ms. Kowalski believed in lots of class participation and always came up with the best questions to ask to get the conversation going. Books and plays that seemed dry and uninteresting came alive in our discussions, opening a whole new understanding of what the author was trying to say.

Ms. Kowalski was waiting at the classroom door this morning. I smiled as I walked by her into class. "Good morning, Ms. Kowalski."

But she looked notably unhappy to see me. "Stop right there, Frank."

I stopped.

Up to that point, I had never heard Ms. Kowalski use a tone stronger than "mildly annoyed." But this morning, she sounded *mad.*

At *me.*

"What's up?" I asked.

She held up a sheaf of papers in her hand. "You're not coming to class this morning. You're going with Mr. Porter here—"

She nodded behind me, and that's when I noticed my guidance counselor, Mr. Porter, approaching from the bank of lockers. *Was he waiting there for me?* I'd met with Mr. Porter exactly once, at the start of the year, to talk about preparing for college applications. Interestingly, he'd found no cause for concern in my lack of extracurricular activities.

"—to talk about *this paper.*"

She held up the papers again. She said *this paper* like she was saying *this piece of dog poop* or *this snot-crusted used tissue.*

"Um," I said, trying to stay calm, "what paper is that?"

"The paper you turned in *last night*, Frank." This time she held up the paper long enough for me to read the cover page.

BLOOD ON MY HANDS:
LADY MACBETH AND THE PROBLEM
WITH WOMEN IN POWER.
BY FRANK HARDY

"Ah—um—"

I had never seen this paper before in my life. Also, I mean, *come on.* "The Problem with Women in Power"? I wasn't some kind of raging, misogynist.

"But I didn't write that!"

Ms. Kowalski sighed and looked at Mr. Porter as though she had expected exactly this reaction.

"It was turned in over our server using your username and password, Frank," Mr. Porter said calmly. "I think we'd better go to the office and talk about this."

We were starting to attract some attention. A small crowd of my classmates was watching, both inside and outside the classroom.

"Dude," Nate Jefferson said, glancing at the paper, "did you seriously *write* that?"

"No!" I said helplessly. "I wrote a paper about the sleepwalking scene! I spent *weeks* on it!"

Ms. Kowalski turned and stomped into the classroom, clearly disgusted with me. I felt horrible. I really *liked* Ms. Kowalski. Now she thought I was some kind of girl-hating monster!

Mr. Porter clamped his hand down on my shoulder. "Let's go discuss this in my office, Frank."

"The thing is, Frank," Mr. Porter said, leaning back in his chair, "even if what you're saying is correct, and this is some kind of setup, it's hard to imagine anyone having the technical skill to pull it off. This paper was turned in at eight forty-five last night, under your name, from a computer at the town library."

"Aha!" I cried. "See, right there, that's wrong! I turned in my paper from home!"

Mr. Porter looked at me skeptically. "Frank, there is no record of you turning in anything from home. There is no record of you turning in anything else, at all."

I tapped my toe nervously. This had to be the work of the masked people. But it was so unexpected. I'd predicted they'd ambush me and bash me over the head, not mess with my schoolwork. Who knew they had a hacker among them? And the school server was notoriously hard to hack into. But clearly, someone had done it. All to target me.

Mr. Porter gave me a quizzical look. "Do you want to tell me more about who might set you up?" he asked. "Is this a problem we can discuss?"

Oh sure. Well, Principal Gerther made my brother and me join the basketball team for some reason we can't figure out, and then these masked people put bags over our heads and drove us to someone's basement, where they tried to brand my brother and promised to ruin our lives if we didn't quit the team. So we didn't, which is a decision I'm starting to rethink, and it looks like they wrote a fake woman-hating paper about Macbeth, *hacked into the school server, and submitted it in my name. And somehow scuttled the actual, amazing paper I spent three weeks writing about the sleepwalking scene.*

"No," I said, looking down at my lap. "It's . . . never mind."

Mr. Porter looked disappointed. "I feel like there must be more for us to discuss, Frank," he said. "If you did write this paper, it's full of anger and disturbing thoughts. You should talk to someone about that."

"I didn't write the paper," I said.

"I wish I could believe you," Mr. Porter said, "but the evidence says otherwise. I'm sorry, but you're going to receive an F on this paper, and I have to give you in-school suspension for two days. Handing such an offensive paper in to Ms. Kowalski is considered an aggressive act."

I took in a deep breath through my nose. "Okay."

Mr. Porter nodded. "You can report to the in-school suspension room, room nine in the basement. I'm sorry, Frank. If you decide there's more you'd like to tell me about this, you know my door is always open."

I thanked him and got to my feet.

Unfortunately, there was nothing more to discuss with Mr. Porter.

But there was a *lot* for me to discuss with my brother.

6 PHOTO BOMBED

JOE

MY FIRST CLASS OF THE DAY IS HISTORY. It's also the only class I have with Marianne, and I was eager to see her. I was still feeling bad about bagging on our plans so I could go to basketball practice, and I wanted to make a date for the weekend so we could catch up.

When I settled into the desk next to her, though, she barely looked at me.

"Hey," I said, reaching out and touching her arm. "Can we make plans for Friday? I've been missing you!"

Marianne looked at me like I was some weird guy off the street. She pulled her arm away and straightened up, glaring down her nose at me. "*Really?*" she huffed.

"Yeah, really," I said, not sure what was going on.

Marianne was usually super mellow and easygoing. Why was she acting like one of the Real Housewives?

"That's not what I've heard," she said, pulling her phone out of her pocket and thrusting it at me.

I looked down at the screen.

What the heck?!

It was a screenshot of a text conversation between "Joe Hardy" and "Lila Derroches." Lila is a cheerleader who basically the entire male student body agrees is cute. She is also way, way out of my league.

JOE: So when are we getting together?

LILA: Are you serious right now?
Thought you were dating Marianne.

JOE: Serious as cancer. I think you're gorgeous.

LILA: What about Marianne?

JOE: What she doesn't know won't hurt her.

I looked up at Marianne, sputtering. "I didn't—I mean, I don't even—"

"Don't try to deny it, Joe," Marianne said sharply. "I also have this."

She took back her phone and clicked around a bit, finally handing it back to me with a photo.

A photo of me and Lila Derroches—her kissing my cheek!

What is going on??

Just to be clear: I've never even spoken to Lila Derroches.

Not via text, not via carrier pigeon, not at all. And I *certainly* haven't gotten a smooch on the cheek from her. If Lila could even pick me out of a lineup, I'd be stunned.

But *someone* sure wanted to make it look like I had. The photo was a fake, obviously, a Photoshop job—but a very good one. I recognized the photo, which was one from my Facebook page of Aunt Trudy giving me a cheek smooch on my birthday. (Is it dorky to love your aunt and not be embarrassed about it? THEN I GUESS I'M DORKY.) Someone had found the perfect photo of Lila Derroches to paste into it, matching the lighting and everything.

I looked from the photo to Marianne. "Look, this isn't me," I said.

She nodded. "Suuuuuuuuuure," she drawled, her disgusted tone making it clear she wasn't sure at all.

"Where did you even get this?" I started clicking around on Marianne's phone, trying to find out, but she snatched it back from me.

"An anonymous e-mail, if you must know," she said. "It was signed 'A Concerned Citizen.'"

"That doesn't seem strange to you?" I asked. "Look, there's a simple solution to this. Ask Lila whether she knows me."

Marianne snorted. "No, there's an even simpler solution to this," she said. "*I break up with you.* Why should I have to ask Lila when there's photographic evidence that you guys have been together?"

"I told you, that's fake!"

Marianne shook her head. She looked really upset now. "Joe, I don't need this negativity in my life. Who would make a fake photo of you and Lila? Who has that much time and energy to spend on breaking us up?"

Funny you should ask. "Actually," I said, sitting up in my chair and putting on my best serious expression, "I've made some powerful enemies over the last couple days, and I think they're trying to set me up."

Marianne looked me in the eye. Her mouth dropped open, and for a second I thought I had her convinced I was telling the truth. I waited for her coo of concern, her expression of support for my bravery in taking on the big guns.

"Are you kidding me?" she said finally. "'I've made some powerful enemies'? I'm sorry, Joe, but I'm going to trust my eyes on this one. We're through."

And with that, she put her phone in her purse, pulled out her textbook, and wouldn't look at me again for the rest of the class.

"You will not *believe* what happened to me," was the first thing Frank said to me when we met up in the lunch line.

"You won't believe what happened to *me*," I replied. "I think the masked people were serious about ruining our lives."

Frank frowned. "You don't say," he murmured, grabbing a ham sandwich from the premade bar. "Okay, I'll bite. What happened to *you*?"

I told him the whole sordid story about Marianne: the

faked screenshots, the Photoshopped picture.

Frank listened with his eyes getting wider and wider. When I finished—we'd paid and were settling into our usual table by then—his eyes were as wide as saucers.

"I guess Marianne won't be joining us, then?" he asked.

I snorted. "Not unless she wants to throw some rotten fruit at me or something," I said. "I think she and I are through."

Frank nodded. "Well, you've had almost as bad a morning as me," he said. And then he told me the crazy story of Ms. Kowalski thinking he wrote this insane, woman-hating paper, and having to talk to his guidance counselor about it, and ending up with an F and in-school suspension.

"In-school suspension is the *worst*," I said. "It has all the stigma of suspension, with none of the daytime TV."

"Amen," said Frank.

"Wow." I sat stock-still, thinking this over. Suddenly my appetite was gone. I pushed my tray away.

"So we can add some attributes to these masked hazers, whoever they are," said Frank. "They have major tech savvy. They must have a hacker among them."

"And they use their skills to *ruin lives*," I said, crinkling my napkin into a little ball. "Frank, this is getting serious. I know you want to defeat these bullies. But I think we have to go to Gerther now—"

"NO!" cried Frank. "Then they win!"

I shook my head. "Let me finish. We go to Gerther and tell him what's happened. Then we at least get to find out why he wanted us to join the team. You and I both know this isn't really about our lack of extracurriculars."

Frank was quiet, apparently thinking that over. "You've had worse ideas," he admitted finally.

"We need more details," I went on. "Whoever these guys are, they're a formidable enemy. We need Gerther to know how bad this is, and we need all the information he has, if he wants us to solve the problem."

"You're right," Frank said, looking down at his sandwich. "And maybe talking to him will bring my appetite back. Shall we go now?"

I stood and threw my tray into the nearest trash can. I felt bad about wasting the daily special, but we had bigger fish to fry. (Not that the daily special was fish. At least, I didn't think so.)

We lost no time in making our way to the office. Inside, the receptionist was on the phone. We waited patiently, staring at Gerther's closed door. *So he's in there with a student,* I thought.

Finally the receptionist hung up the phone and looked up at us. "Yes?"

"We're here to see Principal Gerther," Frank said.

"I'm afraid that's impossible," the receptionist replied.

"Look," I said, "I don't mean to be rude, but we're not going to take no for an answer. We have something of great importance to discuss with Principal Gerther. It's an *emergency.* Can you tell him that Frank and Joe Hardy are here, and it's urgent?"

The receptionist blinked at me, unimpressed. "I'm sorry, I can't do that, young man."

"Why *not*?" asked Frank. "Don't tell me he told you not to let us in. Did he tell you not to let us in?"

Now the receptionist turned and blinked at Frank. "May I suggest that you two cut down on the caffeine?" she asked. "To answer your question, I can't do that because Principal Gerther is *out* today. He took a personal day. Now, would you like to leave a message for him?"

A personal day? I looked at Frank. I could tell he was thinking the same thing I was. *Principal Gerther has a life?*

"No," said Frank, looking a little sheepish. "We'll, uh, come back tomorrow."

"He's out tomorrow, too," the receptionist said, turning back to her computer. "Try the day after."

"Okay, the day after," Frank said.

He looked at me and nodded toward the door. I wished I hadn't thrown away my lunch. What was I going to do for the next twenty minutes until the bell rang?

Then I saw a familiar face stalk into the office and take a quick right, into the mailroom.

Coach Perotta.

I nudged Frank and pointed at him. Frank looked, then turned back to me, eyes wide.

"Coach Perotta," he whispered, stating the obvious.

"Why didn't we think of talking to him?" I whispered back.

Frank shrugged. "I'm not sure. I guess it's possible he already knows about the hazing."

"But if he *doesn't*," I hissed, "he *should*. And maybe he

can help us figure out who's behind it."

We both turned and watched as Coach Perotta left the mailroom, carrying a stack of papers and whistling a cheerful little tune.

Frank cleared his throat. "Hi, Coach Perotta," he said loudly, planting himself in the big guy's path. "Can Joe and I talk to you privately for a minute?"

Coach Perotta looked a little wary at first, but he agreed to chat with us and led us all the way to his private office in the gym.

"Have a seat," he said, gesturing to two folding chairs and walking around his desk to sit down himself.

We sat.

I looked at Frank.

"Um, I guess you're wondering—" Frank began, but Coach Perotta held up a hand to stop him.

"I have a feeling I know why you're here," he said, in a resigned-sounding voice.

"You do?" I asked, surprised.

The coach nodded. "Listen, I know the last couple of days haven't been easy for you boys," he said, sitting up a little straighter in his chair. "And I want you to know . . . you shouldn't be ashamed for coming to me like this."

Frank and I looked at each other. *Huh?* "Oh, we're not," Frank said.

"My dad used to tell me, 'There's no shame in knowing when you're beat,'" Coach Perotta went on.

"Huh," I said thoughtfully. "Well, I guess, in a way—"

"Not everybody can be good at everything," Coach Perotta went on. "Not everybody is cut out for lab work. Not everybody can star in a Broadway show. And certainly, not everybody is cut out for basketball. And sometimes, quitting isn't a cowardly act. Sometimes quitting is the bravest thing you can do."

I was beginning to figure out where this was going. "Coach Perotta," I said, "I'm sorry, but we didn't come here to quit."

"You didn't?" The coach looked from me to Frank, his mouth tightening with annoyance. "Then why *are* you here?"

"We had something else to ask you about," Frank said. "Er . . . have you ever had any trouble with *hazing* on the team?"

Coach frowned. "Hazing?" he asked. "You mean when they make you drink antifreeze, that kind of thing?"

"Uh, something like that," Frank replied.

Coach's expression suddenly went cold. He paused. "Absolutely not," he said. "Hazing is not tolerated on my team, and I make my expectations very clear to my players. Anyone caught hazing would be kicked off immediately, no questions asked."

"Really?" I asked.

"Really," he said, turning his angry gaze on me.

"You've never . . ." I paused, choosing my words carefully. "You've never heard of a masked group forcing team members to do certain things? Play better? Especially the players who are struggling?"

Coach Perotta's nose wrinkled. He suddenly looked disgusted, like I was describing something indecent. "What are you saying, exactly, boy?"

I glanced at Frank, who nodded slightly. I went on to tell Coach Perotta the whole sordid story of what had happened to us on the night we'd tried to join the team for pizza at Paco's. The bags over our heads, the car trunk, the pedestal, the punches, the "brand." The apparent promise Frank and I made to quit the team, and everything that had happened to us this morning after we *hadn't* quit.

Coach Perotta leaned back in his chair and listened, not taking his eyes from mine. Sometimes he looked surprised, sometimes he looked horrified, but he didn't say anything, and he didn't ask me to stop. When I finished, he sat in silence for a moment.

Then suddenly he sat up and roared, "ARE YOU *KIDDING* ME?!"

I jumped, startled. "Sir?"

He lunged across the desk, pointing a finger in my face. "Do you expect me to believe this hogwash? This elaborate lie?"

"Coach Perotta, why would we lie, sir?" Frank asked, sounding as surprised as I was.

The coach turned to him. "Why would you lie?" he asked. "I don't know. Possibly because my contract is up for renewal this year, and I'm coaching potential state champions? You expect me to believe that it's a coincidence Principal Gerther told me I had to add you boys to the team, and then you come back with these outlandish stories of *hazing*? Stories I've *never* heard the like of before?"

There was a knock on the door then, and I felt a shudder of relief. *Please, someone come in and break this tension.* I wasn't sure what reaction I'd been expecting the coach to have, but this definitely wasn't it.

"Come in," Coach Perotta called, and the door opened to reveal Assistant Coach Noonan. From the concerned looks he swept over me and Frank, I got the sense he must have heard Coach Perotta yelling.

"I just came to drop off these stats from the last game," he said, holding up a manila folder. "Is there . . . something I can help with?"

Coach Perotta dropped his head into his hands and then rubbed his temples with his fingers, like Frank and I had given him the world's worst headache. "Have you ever heard of a hazing problem on our team?" he asked quietly.

Coach Noonan frowned. "Hazing? Like at a college fraternity or sorority?" he asked.

Coach Perotta nodded. "Players being forced to do things they don't want to do, humiliating or painful things, to stay on the team. Have you ever heard of anything like that?"

Coach Noonan looked at him for a moment, like he might be missing something, then shook his head. "No, never."

Coach Perotta gestured at us. "Frank and Joe here say they had a very interesting experience with some of our players the other night. Why don't you tell him, boys?"

Coach Noonan looked at me, and I briefly told him the same story we'd just told Coach Perotta.

Coach Noonan paled visibly when I got to the part about the branding.

When I finished, Coach Perotta asked, "Now does that sound familiar at all?"

"No way," Coach Noonan said. "But if there's any possibility our boys are involved in something like that . . . we'd better have a talk with them, hadn't we?"

Coach Perotta looked nonplussed. "What kind of talk?"

Coach Noonan shrugged. "Well, after the next practice, we can sit them down and make it very clear that no hazing will be tolerated on this team. Anyone caught involved in any hazing will be booted off, no questions asked."

Coach Perotta nodded slowly. "Yes," he said after a few seconds, "that sounds reasonable to me. What do you think, boys? If we have a stern chat with our players—is that enough for you to feel comfortable staying on the team?"

Can a stern talk be enough? I thought. I remembered Gabe saying he wouldn't wish the hazing he'd gone through on anybody. I remembered the pizza delivery guy saying this was the third time this month he'd found kids with bound hands and feet and bags over their heads in his parking lot.

"All right," said Frank, and I nodded too.

I guess it's a start.

7 MISUNDERSTOOD

FRANK

OE AND I DID NOT RETURN HOME IN THE best of moods that afternoon. It was a rare day with no basketball practice and no game, so my plan was to crawl into bed and not get out until seven the next morning.

Instead Dad met us at the door. That was unusual. “Hello, boys. Can we speak in my office for a moment?”

I glanced at Joe. “Um, sure.”

Thus far we hadn’t shared any of our basketball-related adventures with our dad. It’s not like we were trying to hide anything from him; we just usually try to leave him out of the crazy complications of the cases we take on. Our dad is a pretty well-known retired detective, and Joe and I inherited the sleuthing gene from him. But we’ve gotten in enough trouble over the years to realize that the less our family gets involved in our mystery-solving problems, the better.

That doesn't mean our dad doesn't know we solve mysteries. He does. And he tries not to ask too many questions.

But I had a funny feeling that this conversation might have something to do with our current activities.

We followed him into his office and sat down opposite him at his big desk.

"Boys," he began, "I had my tires slashed today while the car was in the driveway."

Groan. "Oh, um, I'm sorry, Dad."

He looked at me. "And I got a call this morning, Frank," he said. "It was from a Mr. Porter. Said you'd turned in some ridiculously offensive English paper and got an F and in-school suspension. I told him, that doesn't sound like the Frank I know."

I felt like I was sinking into the chair. "Um, thanks, Dad."

He nodded quickly and then looked from me to Joe. "Trouble in this family seems to follow a certain pattern. Can I deduce that you boys are working on a case?"

I sighed.

"We are," Joe said. "I'm sorry it's affecting you, Dad."

"I'm not worried about me," he said. "I just hope you're not putting yourselves at risk."

That's when we told him the story of everything that had happened to us this week. The weird meeting with Principal Gerther, the night of the masked men, the game, the paper, and Marianne breaking up with Joe. I told him about our conversation with Coach Perotta, and Coach Noonan's proposal that they talk to the other players.

"A talk?" Dad said. "Do you think that will be enough to stop it?"

"I'm not sure," I admitted. "I feel like when hazing gets this bad, it takes a lot to put an end to it. And it sounds like it's been a problem for a while."

Dad nodded, tapping his lip thoughtfully. "When I was in college," he said, "I decided to try to join the same fraternity your grandfather had been part of. But when I started rush as a pledge, I was stunned by what they wanted the pledges to do. We had to humiliate ourselves, acting as servants to the brothers, making them food, doing their laundry. And there were stories of beatings. . . ." He shook himself, like he was picturing it all now. "I gave up," he said. "I didn't want to be a member of any club that would do that to its members. But one of my good friends rode it out, and later, when he was a brother, he loved to lord it over me, how amazing it was to be a brother in this fraternity."

"That's crazy," Joe said. "He wasn't angry they'd treated him that way?"

Dad shook his head. "Oh no. In fact there's a psychological term for it—the loyalty you feel for an organization that's mistreated you. It's called cognitive dissonance," he said. "Essentially, it's your brain's way of dealing with the fact that you've made some odd choices. Instead of being angry with the people who've mistreated them, people convince themselves that it was all worth it, that they *chose* to experience that punishment in order to get the reward. It's all very strange."

"Strange indeed," I agreed.

Dad looked at us sympathetically. "Are you going to stick with the case?" he asked. "You don't have to. Whatever Principal Gerther had in mind, I can't imagine he knew things would get this bad for both of you."

"We're going to stick with it," Joe said decisively, and I turned to look at him in surprise. Originally, it was me who wanted to defeat these bullies, and Joe who (maybe sensibly, I realized now) wanted to go back to Principal Gerther and quit. "We can't let this go on," Joe added. "And I feel like we're getting close now."

"Just be careful," Dad suggested. "Try talking to more of your teammates. They know the truth, even if Coach Perotta doesn't. And do talk to Principal Gerther when you can."

"Good advice, Dad," I said. "But right now I think I want to crawl into bed and turn off my brain for a few hours."

Joe pulled out his phone. "Wait until I send Gabe an e-mail," he said, frantically typing one out.

"Sent!" said Joe, tapping the send button with his thumb.

"Nice job," I said. "Now, we nap."

I napped hard. *So* hard. I roused myself out of bed when Aunt Trudy shook me and said she'd made lasagna, and then I ate some lasagna, and then I relocated to the couch in front of *Dancing with the Stars* (don't judge, my mom is into it) and napped some more. I was shaken awake by Mom, who was holding out my phone. "I think you have a call, Frank."

I struggled to sit up. It was an unfamiliar Bayport number. "Okay. Thanks, Mom." I swiped right to answer the phone. "Hello?"

"Frank, is that you?"

I struggled to recognize the voice through the layers of sleep that still hung over my brain like a fog. "Uh . . . yes."

"Max Crandal here."

Max . . . Crandal. *Oh.* Max *Crandal!*

"Hey, Max, what's up? Listen, I'm really sorry I had to bail on the assembly the other—"

"Yeah. Yeah, listen, Frank. Did you know there was a practice this afternoon?"

I racked my brain. *Practice?* Oh shoot. Yes. It was Wednesday.

"Omigod, Max. I'm really sorry. I just totally bla—"

"Frank, listen. I think you're a nice guy and all, but I don't think you're cut out for the B-Sharps. We had this new freshman join this week, his name is Kyle? And he took over your 'Lion Sleeps Tonight' solo. I just . . . I think he's a better fit for us. Sorry, Frank. Maybe you can try out again next year."

Click.

He'd hung up.

I stared at my phone.

This is what it feels like when your dream dies.

That's when Joe came barreling down the hallway from his room. "Frank! *Frank!*"

"In here!" I yelled.

Joe came running in, holding his own phone in front of him. He ran over to the couch and shoved his phone into my face. "Check it."

The screen showed a text from "Gabe Zimmerman."

brett is willing to talk to you guys about what happened to him. but we should meet soon before he changes his mind. see you at meet locker in 10?

I jumped up. "Text back 'yes,'" I said, fishing for my shoes under the couch. "We can be there in five, even."

"Way ahead of you," Joe said, scrolling down on his phone to show his reply:

see you there.

8

JOE

THERE WAS NOWHERE TO PARK IN FRONT of the Meet Locker, a local diner and hangout, so I ended up parking down Farragut Alley, this tiny little dead-end street off to the right.

It was nine thirty by the time we parked the car, and the Meet Locker closes at ten. "We'd better hurry," I told Frank. "We want to have time to hear everything he has to say."

We jumped out of the car and were heading back out of the alley toward Main Street when suddenly Gabe was standing in front of us.

"Hey!" he said, moving toward us. "Listen, bad news, guys. Brett got cold feet. He doesn't want to hang out in the Meet Locker, in case anyone from the team sees us."

I stared at him. "Ooookay," I said. "So, now what?"

Gabe gestured behind us. "His cousin has an apartment over here," he said. "Just follow me."

There are no streetlights on Farragut Alley, so keeping Gabe in our sights was a little difficult. We followed him down toward the dead end, and then suddenly a door opened to our right, in one of the nondescript retail buildings. I wasn't aware of apartments being inside, but maybe above the stores . . .

"JOE!" Frank suddenly yelled behind me, but it was too late. A dark shape advanced on us from inside the doorway, and a bag was thrown over my head again. I could hear them doing the same to Frank, too. I felt arms reach out and roughly pull me inside.

"I'm sorry," I heard Gabe say behind me, just before it sounded like he was grabbed too.

It felt like there were people on either side of me again, and just like before, they forced me down a short flight of stairs. This time I was led over to a chair and told to sit, and then I felt them tying me to the chair at my waist and my ankles. They tied my wrists together too. When the bag was pulled off my head, I was staring into the same scenario as before: a dark room, black light. This time, though, I was sitting next to not just Frank, but a whole row of guys. When I looked closer, I could just barely make out Pete Gruner, Ty Coolidge, and Jayden Speck.

Just like before, a line of masked, robed figures stood before us. But this time there seemed to be even more of them. The figure in the center moved forward and began to speak.

"Congratulations." Like the last time, he was using a voice modulator to disguise his voice. The sound was low and creepy—like something you'd hear at a haunted house. *"The five of you are the lowest performers on the basketball team. None of you are cut out for basketball. Until you either prove your worth or quit, the harassment will not stop."*

I swallowed and glanced over at Frank. *What form will that harassment take tonight?* I remembered that masked guy advancing on me with the burning-hot pin and felt a shiver run down my spine.

Another masked figure stepped forward. *"We have some fun games planned for tonight,"* he announced, again using a voice modulator. This figure's chosen voice sounded like a creepy child. *"But before we begin, would anyone like to try to prove their worth to the team and bypass the games?"*

"Prove our worth to the team? What does that mean?" I asked.

"It means," the masked figure replied, *"that we're recruiting an assistant for the night. If you want to cross sides and work with us, you'll be exempt from the punishment we plan to exact on your fellow losers. There's only one catch."*

"What's the catch?" Ty asked.

The masked figure cackled. *"You'll find out when you volunteer."*

There was silence for a moment. Surely no one would

volunteer, I figured. Who knew what the catch was? And who wanted to work *with* these guys?

But then a voice spoke up from my left. "I'll do it."

I turned. It was Jayden speaking.

The masked figure chuckled again. *"Very well,"* the figure said. *"Brothers, untie him."*

Two other masked figures came forward and untied Jayden, raising him to his feet.

"Excellent," said the center figure. *"Jayden, you are one of us now. You will help us knock some sense into your fellow losers. And to prove your loyalty, you will let us take a video of you doing it, so we can turn you in if you ever turn on us."*

Frank spoke up next to me. "Don't do it, Jayden!"

One of the masked figures bolted forward and hit Frank in the face before any of the rest of us could react. Frank moaned.

Jayden looked at him, then turned toward the center figure. "I'll do it."

"Very good." The center figure moved forward again, as one of the other figures produced a small video camera and began filming. He kept the camera carefully trained on Jayden. *"Now, it's time for our first game. It's called Run the Gauntlet. Each of the four of you will have to run through a line of masked team members. We are allowed to do anything we like to you—punch you, kick you. This is your punishment for underperforming. Or perhaps"*—he turned his masked face toward Frank and me—*"just being a nuisance."*

Pete leaned forward. "How long do we do this?"

The center figure laughed. *"What an intriguing question. How long do you think you'll do this?"*

Pete looked confused. He shrugged. "Uh . . . once?"

The masked figure laughed again. *"Adorable. You'll do it until we tell you to stop. Until we feel you've learned your lesson. And just looking at the faces in front of me . . . I'd buckle your seat belts, boys. It's going to be a bumpy night."*

I glanced at Frank. *Great.* But punching and kicking, I could take. At least this wouldn't involve burned flesh.

The leader gestured to the other masked figures. Four came forward and began using pocket knives to untie Frank, Pete, Ty, and me from our chairs. Then they began to arrange themselves in two rows, six figures on each side. In between, they left just enough space for a person to pass through.

"Jayden," said the lead figure, *"take your place in the middle, please."*

Jayden looked at us—the poor unfortunates left in the chairs—then quickly looked away. He walked over to the middle of the first line and took his place.

"You are absolutely not allowed to go easy on the losers," the lead figure said. *"If we see you beating them with anything less than your full power, you will be forced to Run the Gauntlet with them, and we will also post the video on your Facebook page."*

Jayden shuddered. He looked straight ahead, carefully avoiding eye contact with both us and the masked figures. I couldn't believe he was going along with this, but at the same time, I didn't feel like I could judge him. Maybe he'd been through more than one of these hazing sessions. Maybe he knew how bad they could get.

"Ty, you're up first," the lead figure said, taking his place at the end of the line.

Ty stood slowly. He glanced back at us, then held his head high, loping toward the two lines.

He paused just briefly at the entrance to the "gauntlet."

"Begin," said the lead masked figure.

Ty stepped into the middle of the masked figures. Immediately, they all fell on him, punching him, kicking him, beating him as if he'd stolen their girlfriends and then hit their mothers. I felt sick, watching and knowing I'd soon face the same.

"Why doesn't he fight back?" Frank whispered.

"You're not allowed," Pete said quietly. "If you do, they beat you even harder next time."

"Next time?" I asked. "How long does this go on?"

"Last time we got out around one a.m.," Pete whispered.

I felt even sicker.

Finally Ty emerged on the other side of the "gauntlet" line. He was hunched over, holding his stomach, but he walked with what little dignity he had left back to his seat.

The lead masked figure stepped out of the line again. *"Just as a reminder,"* he said, *"any one of you can avoid this punishment by quitting the team and preventing us from having to carry your sorry butts."* He paused. *"Any takers?"*

I looked over at Frank. I knew he wouldn't say yes, and I didn't really want to anyway. I just needed to see the determination in his eyes. He sat up straighter and jutted out his chin in defiance.

"Very well," the lead figure went on. *"Pete, you're next. . . ."*

FOUL PLAY

9

FRANK

ND SO I'LL SAY IT ONE MORE TIME, hazing has no place on this team or any team." Coach Perotta folded his arms in front of him as he looked around at each guy sitting on the floor of the gym in front of him.

I turned to glance at Joe, but even the tiny movement hurt. After running the gauntlet four times last night, every muscle in my body ached. The masked hazers had been careful—all my bruises and cuts were on my torso, so none of the damage was visible to the coaches. But practice was going to be *torture* today. It was a huge relief to get to sit down first and listen to this lecture about hazing.

I looked at Gabe, who was sitting behind me and to the right. Just like he had since we got here, he refused to meet my eye. In fact, no one else on the team looked the least bit uncomfortable at Coach Perotta's speech—not even Jayden, Ty, or Pete.

Neither Joe nor I had said anything to Dad about what happened last night. We knew what he would say: it's time to quit. But we were way too infuriated to quit. What was happening on the basketball team was out of control. Someone had to do something!

We'd cornered Ty, Pete, and Jayden separately that morning, trying to talk about last night and what we could do about it. But they all made it clear that none of them were willing to come forward.

"I've put in a whole season with this team," Ty said. "I'm getting better and better. We just have to pay our dues."

"This isn't *paying your dues*, dude," Joe had said. "This is getting beat up by twelve guys while someone videotapes it. Big difference!"

"Nothing that's worth doing is easy," Ty had countered. "That's what my dad says."

I don't think he'd apply it to this situation, I wanted to say. But after talking to Pete and Jayden, it became clear that there wasn't going to be any reasoning with these guys. They were totally drinking the hazing Kool-Aid.

Gerther was the natural next stop. But he was out today, just like the receptionist had said. I was pretty sure Gerther hadn't taken a day off the entire time I'd been at Bayport High. Why had he chosen to start now?

"All right," Coach Perotta said. "Now that we're all on the same page, let's start practice."

Practice. I got to my feet, but even that was a struggle.

We were doing layup drills and I was stinking up the joint, as usual. It got to the point where no one said anything when I got to the front of the line and (inevitably) missed the shot—Coach Perotta stopped offering tips or encouragement, and my teammates just shook their heads helplessly. I was, honestly, too sore to care, and I just wanted to make it through practice in one piece.

Ty and Jayden, though, were really on fire. They were both making shot after shot.

"Amazing job, dude!" Jason said when Ty made his sixth layup in a row.

"Seriously," Dorian said. "From yesterday's practice, it's like night and day. I guess Jason won't have to carry the team anymore!" He laughed, and Jason chuckled a little too.

"That's enough, guys," Assistant Coach Noonan put in from the sidelines. "Though I'm glad to see Ty and Jayden showing such improvement today. See guys—practice makes perfect!"

Is it practice, I wondered, *or having the poop scared out of you?* And if it *was* having the poop scared out of you, what did that say about the hazing—that it was working? Did that make it okay? *No,* I thought, stretching my back and feeling little spikes of pain radiate down my spine. *Nothing would make what we went through last night okay.*

We went into a practice game. Just like in a real game, no one threw the ball to me or Joe, so we just kind of ran around following the action, which was fine with me. Dorian and Jason pulled off a complicated play where they passed the ball down the court using a series of distractions and fake-outs. At the end, though, Jayden was blocking Jason from making the shot, so Jason tried to pass the ball to Pete, who was just a few yards away, so he could get into a better position.

But the ball bounced off the back of Pete's hand. Jayden intercepted it and began dribbling the ball toward the other basket.

Coach Perotta's whistle split the air, and he yelled that that was enough—we could all head to the showers.

Relief flooded through me. *I survived another practice!* And now I got to take a shower, go home, and die on the couch, which was all I wanted in the world.

But as I met up with Joe and walked back to the locker room, I couldn't help but notice Jason walking up to Pete and whispering something in his ear.

Was it just my imagination, or did Pete turn pale?

Jason grinned and walked away, heading toward the locker room himself. Pete lingered for a moment in the same spot, then turned and walked slowly toward Coach Perotta, who was just outside his office. As I watched, Pete said something to the coach, who nodded and led him into his office.

HAZED AND CONFUSED

10

JOE

WE WERE CHANGED AND READY TO leave when Coach Perotta called the entire team back out of the locker room.

"Come back here and sit your butts down," the coach said, his voice nearing a growl. "There's something we need to talk about. *Right* now."

I glanced back at Frank, who was rubbing his shoulder.

"You saw Pete talking to him, right?" I whispered.

Frank nodded. "Right after Jason said something to *him*," he said.

"Do you think he told him everything?" I asked.

Frank shrugged, then winced. "I don't know. Could it be that easy?" he asked.

From the way Coach Perotta was glaring at all of us as

we sat down, I didn't have a good feeling about this. Coach Noonan was standing behind him, and beside him was a shell-shocked-looking Pete. Coach Noonan put his hand on Pete's shoulder as Pete seemed to sway nervously.

"I've just had a private meeting with Pete," Coach Perotta said, slowly scanning everyone's face with a look of disgust. "He's told me some very upsetting things. Things that seem to corroborate something Frank and Joe told me yesterday."

He caught my eye briefly and looked just the tiniest bit sorry. I looked back in disbelief. *Really?*

"I spoke to you earlier today about hazing because I didn't want to believe we had a problem on this team," Coach Perotta said. "No one has ever said a word about it to me. And I hope you all know how I feel about hazing. It's a disgusting, cowardly, unsportsmanlike thing to participate in. Not to mention, if the word ever got out that this was happening on this team, it would disqualify us for any championships. Everything you boys have been working so hard for all winter, gone. Not to mention, the seniors who've won sports scholarships could lose them." He shook his head, clearly appalled. "But it seems like some things have been happening after hours that I had no knowledge of. And worse, these cowardly players have been wearing masks and disguises, going to absurd lengths to keep their identities secret." He paused and glared at us, looking from face to face like he was holding each team member personally responsible.

Coach Noonan spoke up. "Will any brave boys come forward and tell us anything they know about who's behind these incidents?"

All the players seemed to pause and look around at one another uncomfortably. I wondered how many of them knew the true identities of the masked players. Maybe only the masked players themselves knew.

"Come on," said Coach Perotta, unable to hide his impatience. "This is too important to pretend you know nothing. The future of the team is at stake."

More silence. Then suddenly, after a minute or two of awkward shifting, Dorian stood up.

"Coach Perotta," he said, "I don't know who the hazers are, but I have something you should see."

He walked up to Coach Perotta and pulled a smartphone out of his pocket. Pressing the screen with his finger, he started what sounded like a video. Coach Perotta watched, his expression going from curious to angry, and I recognized some of the sounds from the night before.

"*Jayden . . . take your place in the middle, please.*"

I felt my stomach shrivel up. In that video, all the bad guys would be masked. The only visible people would be Jayden . . . and Ty, Pete, Frank, and me.

The video seemed to end, and Coach Perotta took a wobbly step back. His face was flushed red and his nostrils were flaring like an angry bull's. He turned to Dorian. "Where—where did you get that?" he demanded.

Dorian looked a little scared. "It was e-mailed to me from this address I'd never heard of before," he said. "I thought it was a joke."

Coach Perotta grabbed the phone back and began poking at it. "ConcernedCitizen@anonymous.com," he read.

"That's right," said Dorian.

Coach Perotta looked up at the team sitting before him, and his gaze hardened as he settled on me and Frank. "Frank, Joe, and Ty . . . *why* am I just seeing this now?!" he thundered.

"What do you mean?" Frank asked. "We came to you yesterday and told you about the masked guys!"

Coach Perotta shook his head, clearly furious. "No. Why am I just seeing *this* now? This video is time-stamped last night," he yelled, gesturing back at Dorian and his phone. "Why did none of you come forward to tell me this had happened? You know how I feel about hazing on my team!"

Because . . . we weren't sure whether you were in on it? I thought. Even now, I couldn't tell whether Coach Perotta was really horrified by the hazing, or horrified that the hazing had been discovered. I had a feeling that answer wouldn't fly, though.

Frank looked around and slowly—with effort—got to his feet. "Coach Perotta," he said, "you need to know that video is misleading. What *actually* happened is that a whole crew of masked team members hazed me, Joe, Jayden, Pete, and Ty last night, and offered Jayden a way out if he allowed himself to be filmed hazing the others. We might be the only ones visible on the video . . . but we're the victims."

Coach glared at him. "That's all fine and good, but the fact is, the video shows five team members recognizable on camera: Frank, Joe, Ty, Pete, and Jayden. Bayport High has a zero tolerance policy on hazing, and only Pete came forward to report it. That means Jayden, Frank, Joe, and Ty are off the team."

There was an audible gasp from the whole team. "No!" cried Steve. And Ty shook his head, saying, "This can't be. This can't be."

But Coach Perotta didn't falter. "And," he said, "because Jayden is on camera hazing, he will be brought before Principal Gerther and put up for suspension."

"But he was one of the victims!" I cried. "They set him up! They said he could avoid the abuse if he helped abuse the others—but they had to film him, so they had a scapegoat! You're playing right into their hands!"

Coach Perotta turned his hard stare on me, and for a minute my blood ran cold. Dude could be really scary when he wanted to be.

"I have to uphold the rules," he snarled. "If anyone wants to come forward with the masked guys' identities, they can. But for now, I'm doing what I can to stop this."

Frank shook his head. "But that won't stop anything! You're only punishing the victims!"

Coach turned to him, his eyes burning with anger, and

exploded. "*You listen to me!* You and your brother can't come in here and tell me how to run my team after three days! Everything was fine before you Hardy boys showed up!" He threw his arm toward Frank, and for a minute I thought he was actually going to hit him. Instead he pointed, from Frank to me. "You're out! Both of you! *Get out of my gym!*"

Frank looked nervously back at me, and I stood and began walking to the door. Coach didn't have to tell me twice. Heck, it was kind of a relief to have official orders to get out of here.

Frank, Ty, and Jayden followed, each carrying bags with their things. When we got outside the gym, I turned back to face them all. Ty and Jayden looked miserable. They were both staring at the ground.

"We can't let this happen," I said. "We all know what really went down last night. There has to be some way to get the real culprits punished!"

"How?" Jayden looked up at me and shrugged. "The hazing's been going on all season, but no one knows who's really behind it. I've heard rumors that maybe it's Jason, but there's no proof—there's a reason they all wear masks."

Ty hoisted his bag higher on his back. "Frankly, I should've known something was up when the nosy Hardy boys joined the team out of nowhere. You two always say you want to help, but you didn't help anyone here, did you?"

He stomped off, and after a few seconds, Jayden followed.

I looked at Frank. He looked completely, totally miserable.

"What's going on?" a female voice asked from behind me. "You guys look like someone ran over your puppy with a garbage truck."

That's an oddly specific comparison. I turned to see Kelly Pritzky. She was carrying a big gym bag—the girls' team had practice after ours—and wearing a concerned expression.

"Oh, uh, it's nothing," I said. And then I realized, if hazing was such a problem on the boys' team, could it be happening on the girls' team too? "There's this . . . hazing thing happening on the boys' team. We actually just got kicked off because of it."

Kelly looked at me like I was nuts. "*You guys* were hazing people?"

"No." Frank shook his head adamantly. "We were the victims. But it sort of doesn't matter."

"Why doesn't it matter?" Kelly scrunched up her eyebrows.

"Because we're off the team," I said, "and it's someone else's problem to solve now. See you around."

We started walking, and Kelly watched us go. "See you around," she said quietly. Then, when we were a few yards away, she called, "Hey! Was Jason involved? In the hazing, I mean?"

I turned around. "Why do you ask?"

She shrugged. “His scholarship, you know. He’s like a superstar. I’d hate . . .” She trailed off.

“We don’t know whether he was involved,” Frank said. “He’s not in trouble, though. We are.”

Kelly nodded slowly. “I’m sorry,” she said. She looked sincere.

“It’s cool,” I said. “Basketball was never our sport.”

With that, Frank and I walked out of the building and turned toward the parking lot.

“Let’s go home,” he said. “Maybe Aunt Trudy made lasagna.”

“Not likely,” I pointed out. “She made lasagna last night.”

“Don’t kill the last hope I have, okay?”

We walked down the long row toward our car. I was pretty sure we were at our lowest low. We’d persevered so long, we’d made the coaches aware of the problem, and somehow it had all blown up in our faces. The good guys got punished, and evil won.

I was pretty sure we couldn’t feel any worse until we got to our car.

Someone had slashed all four tires.

11 TEAM PLAYERS

FRANK

JOE WAS RIGHT. AUNT TRUDY HAD NOT made lasagna again.

She *had* made her famous turkey meat loaf, which was almost as exciting. I had three pieces.

"And then," Joe was saying as I cut my third piece, "he says that Jayden has to go before Principal Gerther to talk about suspension." He shook his head. "It's like, unreal. It was like this totally dystopian society."

Mom had looked notably unpleased while listening to this whole story. "Well, listen," she said, forking a brussels sprout, "I'm sorry this has been such a horrible case for you, but honestly, I'm glad you're off it. Whatever Principal Gerther was trying to accomplish, I can't imagine he knew it would get this bad."

"If you still need extracurriculars," Aunt Trudy added,

"maybe you can join the Culinary Society. I can always use some hands in the kitchen."

"Speaking of Principal Gerther," my dad said, "do you think I can invoice him for eight new tires?" He'd very nicely picked us up from school that afternoon and arranged to have the car towed and new tires installed.

I wanted to match his light, jokey tone, but the truth was I was too depressed to even answer.

Yes, it was a relief to be off the basketball team, especially since I really stunk at basketball even before I was being beaten up on the regular. And *yes*, it was good to think that we'd escape further harassment now, because we'd finally done what the masked hazers wanted and left the basketball team—though technically, I guess, we were kicked off.

But I *haaaaaaaaaaate* to leave a case unsolved. And we still didn't know what was really happening on the team. Was Coach Perotta in on the hazing or not? Was Jason Bound really pulling the strings, trying to protect his scholarship by any means necessary?

Later that night, I sat at my desk, supposedly working on some extra credit to save my grade in English, but really staring into space and pondering the unfairness of the universe. That's when the phone rang. It was the house landline, which has this ridiculously loud, old-school ring.

"Frank!" yelled Mom from the living room. "It's for you!"

Who would call me on the landline? Had I won a cruise to

the Bahamas? Had my ancient granny decided it was time for a semiannual check-in?

"Hello?" I said.

"Frank Hardy?" a male voice replied. "This is Principal Gerther."

It took me a minute to recognize the voice, because on the phone, apparently, our principal doesn't yell. "Principal Gerther!" I said with the same excitement that a six-year-old might have used speaking to Santa Claus. "We've been trying to reach you!"

"Frank, I feel terrible," Gerther went on. "I've been in the Poconos for my annual reunion with some of my buddies from 'Nam. I got home today and had about five messages from Coach Perotta. He's explained the whole situation to me, and I . . . well, I feel I may have put you and Joe into a situation that was much worse than I thought."

"That's okay, Principal Gerther," I said, though it wasn't. I was still covered in bruises. I was just feeling generous because the possibility of *answers* lurked ahead. "Could we, maybe . . . *talk* to you about it? I think Joe and I would love to know what you know. We're just . . . kind of confused about the whole thing."

"Of course, of course," said Gerther. "Are you free now? I could meet you at the Athens Diner. Don't worry about homework. I'll give an explanation to your teachers."

"That would be great, Principal Gerther. See you there in twenty minutes?"

When he agreed and we'd hung up, I felt about fifty pounds lighter. I leaped out of my chair and walked down the hall to Joe's room, where I pushed open the door. Joe was sprawled on his bed, watching an old Muppets movie on his laptop.

Yep, that's how he unwinds.

He looked at me. "What's up?" he asked. "Please don't tell me you want to talk about it. I'm not ready to talk about it."

"Better yet," I said, "We're going to talk about it with someone else. Put on your shoes. We have a date at the Athens Diner."

"With who?" Joe asked.

"Principal Gerther!" I said cheerfully.

I got a brief glance at Joe's flabbergasted face before I closed the door on my way out.

The Athens Diner is the kind of place that's always moderately busy, whether it's six a.m. or eleven o'clock at night. When we walked in, Joe tugged my arm and pointed to a booth in the back, where Principal Gerther's familiar gray hair floated over the back of the bench.

We walked over. Our principal smiled at us. He was wearing a brown velour zip-up lounge suit, which made me feel weird on multiple levels. And sitting in front of him were three slices of lemon meringue pie.

"I ordered you boys pie," he said, sliding two plates across the booth to us. "I think I at least owe you dessert."

"Thanks," Joe said, taking a seat opposite the principal. I slid in next to my brother.

"So," Principal Gerther began, looking from me to Joe. "Joe, I've told your brother, but I just want to stress to both of you how very sorry I am that the two of you got as caught up in this as you did. Oh, that reminds me." He turned to me. "Frank, I got a call from Mr. Porter that you got an in-school suspension for turning in some absurdly misogynistic paper. That doesn't sound like you."

"It wasn't, sir," I said. "I think whoever's behind all the bad stuff on the basketball team set me up."

He nodded gravely. "I'll take care of it."

Joe looked up from his pie. "My girlfriend also broke up with me," he said. "Same reason."

Principal Gerther looked a little confused. "Would you like me to talk to her?"

Joe shrugged, turning back to his pie. "I guess not. But I *would* like to know what you know about what's happening on the basketball team."

The principal put down his fork. "Well," he said, "a couple months ago I got a call from the parents of a boy who'd dropped off the team. They said he wouldn't give them any details, but they had the sense he'd been *scared* off the team—forced to quit to avoid some kind of abuse." He paused. "I didn't think much of it, honestly, because Coach Perotta has such a sterling record. I talked to him about it, but he said the claims were absurd."

I nodded, remembering how the coach had told me he'd heard nothing about any hazing before we came to him. Then I recalled how he paused when I'd asked him. Did that mean he knew? Did that mean he was involved? I looked at the principal. "But then . . . ," I supplied.

Principal Gerther sighed. "But then a sophomore came to me about two weeks later," he said. "He thought a friend of his was being hazed by someone on the basketball team. I looked into it and couldn't get any answers—the boy was either terrified of telling me the truth, or nothing was going on."

Joe had been devouring his pie while intently listening to Gerther's story, but now he'd hit the crust and put down his fork. "So what happened to make you decide to get us involved?"

"It was something I learned from Janitor Ed, actually," Principal Gerther said. "He was cleaning out the boys' locker room and came across one that had been left unlocked. Inside, he found black robes—the kind a judge might wear. And a pile of these strange, homemade plaster masks with—"

"With creepy designs on them?" I asked. "Painted in white?"

Gerther looked at me and nodded. "Bingo," he said. "It reminded me of something the boys' parents had told me—that the hazers wore masks to avoid being identified."

"So what did you do then?" asked Joe. "Is that when you called us?"

Gerther shook his head. "No. I looked up the locker number where Ed had found the masks and robes, and it belonged to one Jason Bound."

Interesting. "The star of the team," I said.

"Yes," said Gerther. "I'll admit, boys, I didn't want to believe he had anything to do with this. But I called a meeting with him and his parents." He paused.

"It didn't go well?" Joe asked.

"It went *terribly*," Principal Gerther said. "As soon as I mentioned the possibility that Jason might know something about a hazing problem on the basketball team, his father reminded me that he is *very wealthy*—he invented the selfie stick, you know—and has access to some *very high-priced* lawyers."

"Did Jason say anything useful?" I asked.

"He didn't get a chance," Principal Gerther said. "His father took over the conversation, saying that he was quite sure Jason didn't know anything, and that if I wanted to accuse his son and jeopardize his scholarship, that I'd better have *very clear* evidence—or it would mean a lawsuit for the school." He paused and scowled. "You know, BHS is still paying off that girl who claimed she found a rat tooth in her daily special from the cafeteria."

"I suspected that the rumor was true," I said. One of the many reasons I think Joe is nuts to order the daily special every day.

Gerther frowned at me. "I'm not at liberty to discuss it further," he said. "My point is, we don't have the money to be sued by David Bound of Bound Industries. Soooo . . ." He held out his hands, indicating the two of us.

"So you had us join the team," Joe supplied.

"Exactly," Gerther said. "I know you boys are good at solving mysteries."

"But you didn't tell us anything about your hazing suspicions," I pointed out. "You sort of sent us in blind."

"I know, and I regret that now," Principal Gerther said, poking at his pie remnants with his fork. "I didn't want to prejudice you. I wanted any evidence you brought to me to be pure enough to stand up in a court of law." He paused, frowning. "But in trying to achieve that, I put you two at risk. You have my sincere apologies for that."

"Accepted," I said. Joe looked at me with a little surprise, but I saw no point in holding grudges. It was clear Principal Gerther now saw just how dangerous the hazing situation was.

"Hey," Joe said suddenly, "you're not yelling anymore."

"Excuse me?" asked Principal Gerther.

Joe was right. "You usually speak at a . . . higher volume," I said. "Sometimes it seems like you might have trouble hearing us."

"Oh." Principal Gerther's eyes widened in recognition. "Well, to be honest, boys, my wife has told me for some time that she thinks I have a hearing loss and should look into a hearing aid. I always resisted, because I didn't want to look like an old fogey. But one of my 'Nam buddies, Herb, showed me this little tiny thing he inserts into his ear every day, that makes everything sound clear as a bell. You can't even see it!" He tapped his ear. "I decided to give it a try."

"Wow," Joe and I murmured at the same time. *A Principal Gerther who admits he was wrong, cares about our well-being, and speaks at a normal volume?* The times they were a-changin'.

We were quiet for a minute, absorbing this news, when

suddenly Joe straightened in his seat. "So what now?" he asked.

"Now," Gerther said, "I think I have no choice but to suspend the basketball team until Coach Perotta can work with me to get to the bottom of this."

"But that punishes the whole team!" I pointed out. "I don't think *everybody* is involved."

"But it seems that everybody is aware," Principal Gerther said. "Everyone knows about the problem, and no one has reported it. That goes against the BHS honor code, right there."

"I think they're afraid," Joe said quietly. "The masked guys are pretty . . . scary."

"And the people who made it through the hazing," I added, "have convinced themselves it was worth the struggle. It's a psychological phenomenon called 'cognitive dissonance.'"

A brief shadow passed over Principal Gerther's face, like he had just remembered I was annoying.

"Listen," I said, leaning forward, "can you just overturn Perotta's punishment and get us back on the team?"

"What?" Gerther asked.

"What?" Joe echoed, looking at me like I was insane.

"Of course I *could*," Principal Gerther went on. "I *am* the principal. But is that really a good idea? I don't want to expose you boys to further risk."

I looked at Joe, trying to use my brother-telepathy to say: *We're so close. Let's just finish this.*

At least some of that must have landed, because Joe turned to the principal with a new sense of determination. "Frank's right," he said. "We're so close to figuring out what's really going on. Let us get to the bottom of this. We'll get you proof. Something incriminating, on film or video."

Gerther looked from him to me, wearing a dubious expression. He shook his head. Finally he said, "All right—but I'm sending you back in with a bodyguard of sorts."

A bodyguard?

"Whatever," Joe said. "As long as you get us back on the team."

"Along with Ty, Pete, and Jayden," I added. *They have a right to play in the championship game they helped get to.*

Principal Gerther nodded. "Consider it done." He looked at us seriously over our near-empty plates. "I feel like up to this point, I've underestimated both of you. You're good boys. Your parents raised you right."

That was awfully nice of him. "Thanks, Principal Gerther." I wanted to add something like, *You're nice too,* but it seemed inappropriate.

"I realize you're doing me a big favor by helping me get to the bottom of this," Principal Gerther added. "Is there anything I can do for you in return?"

I glanced at Joe, who shrugged. *Good,* I thought. *I'll take this one.*

I turned back to Gerther with an eager smile.

"Actually," I said, "is there any way you can get me back into the B-Sharps?"

BODY GUARDED

12

JOE

"GOOD MORNING, BOYS."

About twelve hours after we'd parted from Principal Gerther in the Athens Diner parking lot, he welcomed us back into his office. Coach Perotta, Coach Noonan, Ty, Pete, Jayden, and some huge guy I'd never seen before were seated in folding chairs all around his desk.

"Um, hi," I said, feeling nervous for some reason I couldn't quite place. Last night, I'd totally understood why Frank wanted to get back on the team. He hates to leave a case unsolved, and truth be told, so do I. But now I wondered if we'd glossed over the risks in the midst of our excitement.

Coach Perotta glanced up at us, clearly using all the

energy he had to stifle a scowl. He looked about as happy to see us as you would be to see a family of rats move into your kitchen cabinets. Jayden, Pete, and Ty wore more guarded, curious expressions. And the huge guy weighed at least two-fifty and had a five o'clock shadow at nine thirty in the morning. Was he someone's big brother?

"I've been talking to Coaches Perotta and Noonan about what happened yesterday during basketball practice," Principal Gerther explained. "We think we've reached a decision." He nodded at Coach Perotta.

"Yes," said Coach Perotta, not quite making eye contact with us. "I think in my frustration, I may have acted hastily. I realize now that you all were clearly the victims of the hazing, not perpetrating it. Moving forward, I promise to work *with* you to solve the hazing problem."

"And?" prompted Principal Gerther.

"And," Coach Perotta went on, looking like he smelled something rotten, "you can all return to the team."

Ty let out a whoop of excitement. Jayden and Pete looked pretty thrilled too—if a bit confused.

Principal Gerther indicated the big guy. "And this," he said, "is Owen. Say hello, Owen."

"Hello," said Owen. His voice was as deep as the guys' on these old soul records Mom likes to listen to.

"Owen is a new student here, beginning today," said Principal Gerther. "He's going to join the basketball team too."

Subtle, I thought. But if Ty, Pete, or Jayden thought this was weird, they didn't show it. They were probably too excited to get back on the team.

Frank nudged me. "Owen looks about thirty," he whispered. "He has a five o'clock shadow!"

"Don't look a gift thirty-year-old in the mouth," I hissed back.

Principal Gerther told the coaches, Pete, Jayden, and Ty that they could leave. He asked me and Frank to stay behind, with Owen.

"Owen is your new bodyguard," Gerther whispered as soon as the others were out the door. "I want you to take him everywhere. His only job is to keep you safe."

"What if Frank and I have different classes?" Joe asked.

Principal Gerther seemed to deflate for a moment, but only a moment. "He'll alternate," he said. "He'll start out with Frank, then meet you, Joe, at your locker between classes. Then he'll go to class with you, and vice versa."

It seemed a little complicated to me, but I'd take it. I much preferred Principal Gerther Who Cares About the Hardy Boys' Well-Being to the previous version.

Frank and I met up again at lunch. Owen was trailing me from history class, where he'd asked some surprisingly astute and probing questions about the Boer War.

"So, who are you, exactly?" I asked, wondering if Principal Gerther's 'Nam buddies somehow had access to the CIA.

“I work for Safe ’n’ Sound Security Solutions,” Owen replied cheerfully.

“You’re a rent-a-cop,” I filled in.

“Exactly,” Owen said with a nod. “Do they have a salad bar here?”

“Yes, but you don’t want to eat from it,” I said. “Come with me. Your best bet is the daily special. Anyway, are you armed?”

Owen snorted. “In a high school?” he asked. “No, I’m not armed, but I do have this.” He lifted his shirt, where a rectangular black box was clipped to his belt. A Taser. “If anyone messes with you or your brother,” he said, “they get fifty thousand volts!”

That was comforting, I guessed. I spotted Frank walking up to us in the food line, and we all went through and chose our food.

“The daily special,” Owen told the lunch ladies enthusiastically when it was his turn.

Frank grimaced at me. “I knew you’d turn him into you eventually.”

“What now?” Owen asked after we paid. “Where do you guys usually sit?”

“We usually sit over there,” Frank said, gesturing sort of vaguely to the back of the room, “but today, I think we should spend lunch trying to talk to Gabe Zimmerman.”

Gabe. Frank had a good point. At our last hazing fiasco,

Gabe had lured us there, after seeming like he wanted to help us. He had to know something about who was pulling the strings.

"Good call," I said.

It took us a little while to find Gabe in the lunchroom. We checked out all the usual moderately-popular-sophomore tables before finally locating Gabe at a table in front.

With the popular seniors.

Including Jason Bound.

I gave Frank a quizzical look. *That's weird.* They were on the basketball team together, sure, but Gabe and Jason didn't seem close, nor did they hang with the same crowd.

"Huh," said Frank, watching Gabe with a perplexed expression. "Well, let's see if he'll talk to us."

We walked up behind Gabe, and Frank tapped him on the shoulder. Gabe turned, his eyes widening with recognition at the sight of us—and not the good kind of recognition.

"Can we talk to you privately, Gabe?" Frank asked. "We think we have a few things to discuss."

Jason, who was sitting kitty-corner to Gabe, looked up at us with a cool expression. "Oh, look who it is," he said. "Coach Perotta's *favorite* players."

Had word spread so quickly? "Hey, Jason," I said, trying to look friendly. After all, we didn't have anything against Jason, personally. Nothing that had happened the day before seemed directly related to him.

He just stared back at me, not looking friendly. "I heard Perotta let you back on the team already," he said. "After Principal Gerther basically forced him."

Some other guys from the team, including Dorian, were sitting at the table too. Suddenly I could feel all their eyes on us.

Frank nodded. "Yeah. Coach realized we were the victims in the whole hazing thing, so we didn't need to be punished."

Jason's eyes narrowed. "I just don't get it," he said, cutting his eyes from Frank to me. "Why are you so determined to stay on the team? Why are you trying so hard? You're obviously not basketball players."

It was a good question. "We're trying to prove something to ourselves," I said honestly. "Haven't you ever felt like that before? We don't want to quit."

Jason seemed to take that in, and even gave a little nod. He looked back up at me, his eyes sincere now. "I respect that," he said.

Beside him, Dorian let out a snort. "The only thing you two are proving," he muttered, "is that you're bad basketball players."

Most of the table laughed at that. But Jason was still watching us, thoughtful. He looked at Gabe. "Why don't you talk to them, like they want?" he asked.

Gabe looked a little cowed as he slowly got to his feet. He looked nervously from me and Frank to Owen. "Where do you want to go?"

"Let's just go to the soda machines," I said. We walked over to the wall, where it was quiet except for the hum of the machines.

"What do you want?" Gabe asked. His words were rushed and clipped. He clearly wanted to get this over with ASAP.

"We want to know what you know," Frank replied in a low voice. "You helped lure us to Farragut Alley the night we were hazed with Ty, Pete, and Jayden. So clearly you're in league with whoever's doing this."

Gabe's eyes bugged out. "That doesn't mean I'm *in league* with them," he insisted.

"Then why don't you tell us what happened?" I asked.

Gabe sighed and looked at the floor. "Okay," he said. "I was walking my dog the night you sent that e-mail about wanting to talk to other people who'd been hazed. I hadn't even seen it yet, but I guess someone had. Because all of a sudden someone grabbed me and pulled me into a van with tinted windows. They put a bag over my head, just like when I was hazed, and they said I could cooperate or they'd see to it that I'd get thrown off the team." He paused. "I'm sorry, you guys, I never meant to hurt anyone. I didn't know what they'd do. But I've worked too hard to get thrown off."

I looked at Frank. He shrugged.

"You didn't hear any voices you recognized?" I asked.

"No," Gabe replied. "Even the van, they were using that . . . distorter thing."

"The modulator," I put in.

"Yeah."

Frank let out an annoyed sigh. "Gabe, really, after a year on the team, you don't have any idea who these guys are? No one does? These masked guys just show up and beat everyone, and all of you younger players are just like 'whatever, cost of playing sports'?"

Gabe looked up then, glaring at Frank. "I don't know any more," he said, slowly and deliberately, "but I wouldn't tell you even if I did. Look, I said I was sorry. But why don't you just do what Jason said and quit the team? It's not *your* job to fix this."

"We're not going to quit, Gabe," Frank said.

Gabe sighed. "All right," he began, lowering his voice again. "Then why don't you try to talk to Diego Lopez? I told you before, he up and quit the team really suddenly. There were rumors they'd done something horrible to him, but he wouldn't talk about it. Maybe *you* could get him to talk." He paused, looking back at his table. "But I can't help you anymore."

With that, he scurried back to the table where Jason, Dorian, and the others were waiting.

PANIC AT THE PARK

13

FRANK

"THERE ARE WORSE PLACES TO START," Joe remarked as we watched Gabe take his seat back at the table with the team's star players. "He mentioned that Diego kid before, remember?"

"Who is he, even, though?" I asked, automatically pulling up my phone and opening Facebook. Diego Lopez . . . Diego Lopez. *There you are.* Several Diego Lopezes popped up, but only one was a teenager from Bayport. I pulled up the public part of his profile. He was a medium-size kid with shoulder-length dark hair and dimples. I thought I'd seen him around school before.

"Send him a message," Joe said, so I typed out:

Hi, Diego. I hope this doesn't seem weird, but I've just joined the basketball team and I'm trying to get to the bottom of this whole hazing situation. I heard you might have had a personal experience that was kind of freaky. I'm not trying to get anyone in trouble, but I'd like to hear your story, if you're willing to tell it. It will be 100 percent confidential. Thanks, Frank Hardy.

"Nice," Joe said. "Strong, but not threatening."

"That's my specialty," I replied, hitting the send button.

One element of being back on the basketball team that I'd almost forgotten was that we'd have to *play basketball* again. And we had a home game that afternoon, the last one before regional championships. Tensions were running high, but surprisingly, when Joe and I got to the gym and started changing into our uniforms, not one player said a single mean thing to us. Steve O'Brien even came up to me and told me he was glad Coach P had let us back on the team. Ty and Jayden gave me fist bumps as I settled onto the bench.

I was expecting to stay on the bench for the whole game—just like before. Not only was I arguably the worst player on the team, but now Coach Perotta kind of hated me personally, too. It wasn't exactly a recipe for success. But

I was perfectly happy with that. It's not like I was staying on the team to become a basketball star.

But just after halftime, Xavier Rawlins fell on his elbow and let out a yelp. Coach Perotta called a time-out, turned around, and looked right at me. "Frank, you're in for Xavier!"

"Me?" I squeaked, looking around at the bench. I was the only Frank, though.

"*You,* Frank," Coach Perotta said, pointing to the court. "Remember what I've taught you, okay?"

I stood, glanced at Joe, who was also on the bench (he'd played a little in the first half, though, and hadn't embarrassed himself), and shakily walked toward the sidelines, where the ref was about to start the clock again. I took my position. The whistle shrilled, calling the game back into session.

And then things began to move very quickly, blending together like a dream. Dorian had the ball, and I was playing defense for him, trying to help him get it down the court. Then suddenly he was surrounded and I was clear. He nodded at me and passed the ball. I tried to get as low as I could—like Coach P had shown me—and dribbled it down the court.

I was getting close to the basket. I looked for someone to pass it to, but no one was open. I caught Jason's eye, and he mimed that I should try for the basket myself.

Me? I wanted to say. *Frank Hardy?*

Then I faked right, moved left, and threw it.

AND IT WENT IN!

My teammates erupted in cheers. I could hear Joe and the other guys on the bench chanting, "Frank! Frank! Frank!" It was like something out of a movie. I stood there and tried to soak it all in, and then . . .

"Frank!" Gabe yelled. He was passing the ball to me. And I was up again.

All in all, I probably only played for three minutes or so before Coach P pulled me out. But it felt like an eternity. A perfect eternity. I played *well!* I made *two baskets!*

When I returned to my spot on the bench, in my mind, I returned as a champion.

Bayport won the game, securing our place in the championships. Even Owen had played for a couple of minutes, and he'd done well. When we went back into the locker room to change, everyone was in a good mood.

Jason came up to me as I was buttoning my shirt and slapped my shoulder. Owen, who'd already changed, was waiting for me on the bench nearby. "You were *on fire* out there, Frank," said Jason. "I guess we're lucky Coach let you back on the team."

I could feel myself blushing. "Aw, thanks, Jason. You were good too."

Dorian was just behind Jason, and I half expected him to point out that that was a stupid thing for me to say to the star player. But instead he looked at me with real respect. "I guess you *have* been paying attention in practice," he said. "You're really improving."

I looked at him. "Maybe players who are struggling just need to be given the time and space to improve," I said pointedly. *And not beaten until they can barely move,* I added silently.

Dorian just nodded at me briefly, and then he and Jason walked out together.

On the drive home, my phone dinged. Since I was behind the wheel, I asked Joe to take a look.

"It's a Facebook message from Diego Lopez," he said. "Want me to read it out loud?"

I nodded.

"'Thanks for the note, Frank, but I don't really want to talk about it.'"

"Arrgh!" I growled in frustration.

"If he just sent it, is he online now?" asked Owen, who was in the backseat. We were supposed to drop him off at the bus station, where his car was waiting, on the way home. "Send him another note. Try to convince him."

Joe looked at Diego's message again. "Yep he's online."

"Tell him we only want to help!" I directed Joe. My brother nodded and typed away.

Ding! "'You can't help,'" Joe read aloud.

"Tell him we can't help if no one will talk to us!" I said. Joe typed the message.

Nothing for a couple of minutes.

"Tell him we want to stop this from happening to others,"

I said. My phone was silent until we got to the bus station, and I was beginning to give up hope. We could try to keep bugging Diego, but it would all be useless if he had no interest in telling us the truth. We couldn't *force* him.

But just as I pulled into the bus station lot, my phone dinged again.

I parked the car and grabbed my phone from Joe so I could read it myself.

All right—I'll meet with you.
But it has to be somewhere out of the way,
where no one will see.

Like where? I wrote. *Pick the place, we'll meet you there.*

There was a pause of a few seconds. Then his reply dinged.

There's a baseball field in Waltham Park in Chins River, he wrote back. *Meet me there at ten p.m. Just you two please!!* I showed Joe, then wrote back, *Okay, see you then.*

"A deserted baseball field in a deserted park on a deserted road one town away?" Joe asked. "That sounds like a *great* idea if we're looking to get abducted again."

"But I'll be with you guys," Owen's deep voice intoned from the backseat.

"You will?" Joe asked, turning to look at him quizzically.

"Yeah," I said, turning too. "I thought you were just our bodyguard for school and team events."

Owen shook his head cheerfully. "Nope," he said, "I'm

here for you whenever you need me, day or night, rain or shine. You just say the word. Besides," he added, "Gerther is paying me by the hour."

At 10:02 that night, the three of us sat in our car, in a parking lot by the baseball field at Waltham Park. Our headlights were trained on the field.

"Nobody's here," Joe said, his voice heavy with defeat. "Is this another setup?"

"If it is, I'll keep you safe," Owen said, looking up from his phone, where he was playing a game. "Just hang out for a few minutes. Maybe the kid's just late."

Joe sighed. I stared out the window, willing Diego to show up. *We need answers,* I thought. As much as we knew about the hazing on the basketball team, we still had no idea who was behind it.

Then, finally, at 10:07, a dark red sedan arrived. It pulled into a parking place a few yards away, and then the engine turned off and the driver's-side door opened. A smallish guy got out. I recognized his dimples from the photo on Facebook: Diego.

I looked at Joe.

"I guess it's not a setup after all," he said, looking pleased. We unclipped our seat belts and climbed out, leaving Owen in the backseat.

"Hey," I called to the kid. "I'm Frank, and this is my brother, Joe."

He looked nervous, even though we hadn't seen anyone for miles. "Um, hey. Diego."

"So, Diego," I began, moving closer. "What can you tell us about what happened to you?"

"Well . . . ," Diego said. He was looking around, like he expected to see the masked guys jump out from the woods. "It was a long time ago. . . ."

"This past fall, yeah?" asked Joe.

Diego nodded. "Right, yeah, this fall. I wasn't playing well."

"Were you not playing well like you were playing badly, or were you just new?" I asked. This seemed like an important distinction as far as hazing was concerned.

Diego looked at me. "Um, I was new, I guess." He paused. "Anyway, I . . . They told me to meet them. . . ."

"Who did?" asked Joe.

Diego looked confused now. "It was—they were—"

"Who told you to meet them?" I asked.

Diego looked from me to Joe. *Is this guy for real?* I wondered. I guessed it was understandable for him to be nervous, but this guy was all over the place.

"It was . . . it was Jason who invited me," he said finally. *Jason,* I thought with a frown. I wanted to believe Jason was a nice guy . . . but could it be coincidence that he seemed so involved in setting up the victims? "But I don't know whether he knew what would happen. Maybe he told other people I was meeting him, and they took the opportunity to grab me. He told me to meet him at Athlete's Warehouse, so he could give me advice on what sneakers to buy to help improve my game." He paused again. "As soon as I got out of the car, someone put a bag over my head and shoved me in a trunk. When they took off the bag, it was pitch dark, and there were these guys wearing masks."

Sounds familiar. "Were you the only victim?" I asked.

"No." He shook his head. "I was never the only victim."

"How many times did it happen?" Joe asked.

Diego puffed up his cheeks and then blew the breath out of his mouth. "*Ay*, I dunno. Five or six times, at least. The last time, they hit me so hard they broke my arm."

"They *broke your arm*?" I asked. "Did you tell anyone?"

"No," Diego replied. "Not even my parents. They said they would ruin my life if I told."

Also sounds familiar. "Did you ever have a suspicion about who the guys were?"

Diego looked down. "Not at the time," he said. "But after . . . months after . . . I realized . . ." He glanced up, into the woods. I wondered if he seriously thought someone might be in there, listening. *These guys really did a number on him,* I thought, *if he's this paranoid months later!*

"What did you realize?" Joe prompted. I realized my brother was leaning forward, hanging on Diego's every word. He was as excited by this as I was. *Finally, some answers!*

"I realized . . ." Diego looked from us to the woods again. *Stop it,* I wanted to say, *there's no one listening.* But then suddenly he opened his mouth wide and screamed, "BANAAAAAAAANAAAAAAAA!"

It had to be some kind of code word he'd been told to say, because that's when all hell broke loose.

At least ten guys ran out of the shadows in the woods, dressed all in black, with ski masks over their faces. They were running right for *us*. Diego gave us a grim look and then ran for his car. Within seconds, I heard him squealing out of the lot.

Meanwhile, Owen threw open the back door of our car and came barreling out, Taser sparking. "Hold it right there!" he yelled. "I detain you all on behalf of Safe 'n' Sound Security Solutions!"

But two of the largest guys paused, looked at each other, and then ran right at Owen. Owen screamed and sparked up the Taser, but before he could aim it at them, the larger one reached over and grabbed it out of his hand.

"MY TASER!" Owen yelled, winding up to punch the guy. But he'd lost track of the guy behind him, who calmly pulled a billy club off his belt loop and brought it crashing down on Owen's head.

"Uhhhhh . . . ," Owen moaned, and fell over, out cold.

Oh shoot. I looked at Joe. There went our protection. I looked up to see three guys advancing on me, three on Joe.

"Just fight!" Joe cried, but I could hear the fear in his voice.

I tried my best self-defense moves on the guys, using

their weight to my advantage, aiming for their vulnerable spots. But there were just too many of them. After getting one good jab in at the first one's eyes, I was tackled to the ground and felt the familiar bag going over my head. *Not again . . .*

But what was even more disturbing than the sudden attack was the *whap-whap-whap* sound that started in the distance, but was getting closer . . . and closer . . . and closer.

It sounded like a helicopter landing on the baseball field.

14 HIT AND RUN

JOE

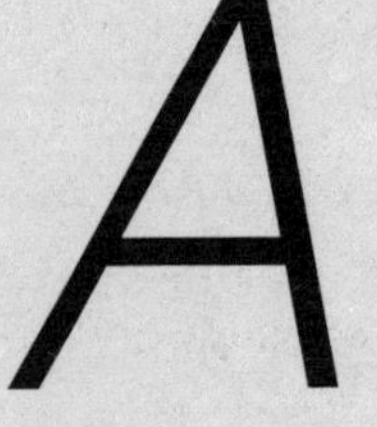

RE YOU KIDDING ME?

I was *not happy* when those guys started streaming out of the woods and Diego took off. I was even less happy when they beat our security guard over the head with a billy club and started running for me and Frank. I was SUPER-DUPER IRRITATED when they threw a bag over Frank's head.

I was SURPREMELY DISPLEASED when I heard the helicopter.

But at least part of my annoyance was with myself. I *knew* the meet-up sounded fishy when Diego said he wanted to talk at an abandoned baseball field one town away.

But I guess I also wanted to believe that Diego was legit.

We needed his story if we were ever going to crack this case. And I wanted to crack this case. Plus, we had our very own bodyguard. What could go wrong?

Oh, just everything.

So when the bag slipped over my head, I wasn't really in a "just cooperate and see where they go with this" kind of mood. No, I kicked upward with all I had in me, and I heard the guy scream and fall. I swung out with my elbows, making contact with at least one of the other guys' skulls, and then I just started running.

I'd gone a few yards by the time I got the bag off my head.

Which was when I looked up to see a huge white helicopter landing on the field with BOUND INDUSTRIES painted in blue letters along the side.

What the heck . . . ?

So this meeting has given us answers. Clearly, Jason *was* behind all this, or at least heavily involved. I grabbed my phone out of my pocket and dialed 9-1-1.

"9-1-1, what is your emergency?"

"Yeah," I said. "I'm at the baseball field at Waltham Park in Toms River, and my brother and I have just been attacked by a bunch of goons in ski masks. They're trying to load us into a helicopter."

There was silence for a moment on the other end of the line. I heard typing. "So just to verify, sir, these goons are in Waltham—"

SLAM! Someone jumped out of the shadows to my

right and tackled me to the ground, knocking the phone out of my hand. No sooner was I on the ground than three or four more people came out of nowhere to jump on top of me. They picked me up by the armpits and dragged me to my feet.

I was facing the copter now, and my blood ran cold when I saw about three other figures forcing my brother into the helicopter. The blades were still rotating—*WHAP-WHAP-WHAP*—and the thing was hovering just a few inches off the ground. It looked like they were loading Frank into the copter to take off—taking him who knows where.

"Wait!" I yelled at the same time one of the goons holding me yelled the same thing.

The person pushing my brother inside looked over, and the one who'd yelled gestured to me. "We got the other one! Wait!"

No voice distortion. I tried to place the person's voice, but no one immediately came to mind. And I didn't have a lot of time to think.

The person on the copter helped the others shove Frank inside. Right before the door closed the person shook his head, yelling, "It'll be even worse punishment for them to be separated!"

Nooooo! I felt my guts go cold. One of the things my dad has drilled into us, if we're going to solve mysteries and put ourselves in danger, is that *you never let them split you up*. We were always safer together. And I felt a visceral sort of horror seeing the door to the cockpit close, knowing my brother was inside and the thing could take off at any second.

It started to rise up from the ground. The wind from the blades was blowing the dust from the baseball diamond around. *Where are they taking Frank?* I had no idea. I wasn't even sure who these guys were, except that one of them had to be Jason.

"Where are they going?" I yelled, and when no one answered, I screamed it again. "WHERE ARE THEY GOING?!"

No one said a word. I felt something harden within me. When the copter was hovering about five feet off the ground, I lunged at the guys holding me, kicking and scratching at their faces, and kneeing another. It wasn't an elegant attack, but it was enough to make them loosen their grip for just a second—which was all I needed. I ran for the copter, pausing over Owen's inert form. He was out cold. A few yards away from him, I spotted what I was looking for. I reached down and grabbed it, shoving it into my waistband.

Then I ran for the copter like my life depended on it—or like Frank's did. It was too late to board, but I could sure as heck make things awkward. I grabbed onto the landing skid.

"*No way are you guys taking my brother!*" I screamed.

The people who'd been holding me had recovered and run over, but soon I was ten feet off the ground, then fifteen.

AAAAUUGH! Looking down, I realized I hadn't quite thought this through. I *hate* heights.

The cockpit door swung open and one of the masked figures came out, carefully climbing down onto the landing skid.

"You freaking psycho," the person shouted, looking down at me, "what on earth are you doing? Do you want to die?"

I just looked up and screamed, "YOU'RE NOT TAKING MY BROTHER!"

"*Aren't we?*" asked the figure, then lifted his foot, placing it just over my right hand.

Oh no. I really didn't think this through. My hands were frozen on the landing skid, so I couldn't reach for anything to help me. I closed my eyes, wondering if I was about to die. *Well, you had a good run,* I tried to tell myself. *Living beyond your teens is overrated.*

But nothing happened. The crunch of shoe-on-knuckle that I had braced for never came.

When I opened my eyes, the masked person had reached down. "Come on, take my hand," the person grunted. "Don't be a hero."

I realized that whoever it was, he was trying to help me into the cockpit.

CAUGHT IN THE COCKPIT 15

FRANK

I CANNOT TELL YOU HOW RELIEVED I WAS TO see Joe climb through the door into the cockpit.

"Joe!" I cried. The abductors had removed the bag from my head once the helicopter took off, but bound my wrists and ankles. It allowed me to see all the people on the copter with me: three masked goons, a middle-aged pilot I didn't recognize, and now, Joe.

They bound Joe's wrists and ankles like they had mine. Then one of the masked figures spoke—and to my amazement, he was using the voice modulator again.

"It's become clear to us that the two of you morons aren't going to give up. You're determined little buggers. So you've left us only one choice: we'll lock you up somewhere no one will find you until BHS has won the state championship."

The state championship? I tried to remember the dates in my head. It was at least two weeks away.

"*Where* are you going to lock us up?" I asked.

The goon who'd spoken looked to the pilot, who chuckled casually, like this was all a mildly amusing lark.

"I have plenty of access to empty warehouses where no one would think to look," the pilot said in a smooth voice. "A couple of kids in chains shouldn't arouse much suspicion on the industrial waterfront. Oh, I do apologize—I haven't introduced myself." He paused and glanced behind him at Joe, then me. "I'm David Bound, and I invented the selfie stick."

"Gee," Joe said, not bothering to hide his sarcasm. "Thanks."

The guy smiled. "And I am also Jason's father."

He turned back to the controls for a moment, then looked back. "My disguised friends, you can probably lose the masks now too. We've won. These boys won't be bothering you anymore."

All at once, the goons in black reached up and pulled off the masks. Joe and I looked around in amazement—they were Dorian, Kelly Pritzky, and Coach Noonan!

I stared at the three of them, openmouthed. Then I realized someone was missing.

"Where's Jason?" I asked. "Was he one of the guys on the ground?"

David laughed. "Oh, Jason would never let us get away

with a stunt like this. He's far too *sportsmanlike*. We've had to keep our whole process secret!"

"Process?" asked Joe. "What process?"

"Well," said David, "I'll take credit where credit's due. My son's talent was evident last year, but I felt that he was held back by the less-talented players on the BHS team. When I talked to Principal Gerther and Coach Perotta about dissuading them from playing basketball, Perotta had the nerve to get all *moral* on me. He said at BHS, everyone has equal access to all the activities. He reminded me that every player had passed tryouts for the varsity team, and said they would improve with time." David snorted. "But as you all well know, student athletes have only so much time to prove themselves! Why, when I was a teenager, I narrowly missed getting a sports scholarship to my chosen university, because they gave all their scholarships to teams that had ranked higher in the state. Can you *imagine*?" He shook his head, still staring out the windshield. "I knew I couldn't allow that to happen to Jason. We have the wherewithal to send him to college, of course, but he works too hard to have his talents overlooked. And it was clear Coach Perotta wouldn't help me. So this year, I came up with the idea to weed out the weaker players and make sure BHS had a winning team, all the better to showcase Jason's talents and make him the star he deserves to be."

"Weed them out by beating and terrifying them," I filled in. "*Hazing* them."

David shrugged. "Whatever you want to call it." He continued. "Anyway, it wasn't hard to convince Assistant Coach Noonan to help me, since it would be easy to frame Perotta for the hazing and then Noonan here would get his job. Noonan recruited Dorian with the promise that he'd get similar treatment next year—the two of them planted masks and robes in Jason's locker to put the blame on him. I knew I could talk the principal out of taking action against his star player. Then, Dorian recruited Kelly, Jason's girlfriend, who hopes to attend Duke with him next year. It wasn't hard to fill out the group with team members."

Jason's girlfriend. I hadn't realized they were dating, since none of the players had mentioned it. They must have kept their relationship quiet.

I looked from Kelly, to Dorian, to Coach Noonan. But none of them would meet my eyes.

At least they have the sense to be ashamed. But that was cold comfort, considering our current situation.

I still have my phone. I realized this all at once and had to stop myself from jumping up and down in my chair. If I could *very* carefully pull it from my pocket, then maybe hit 9-1-1 without anyone seeing . . .

Suddenly Kelly yelled, "Frank! None of that." She leaned over and grabbed my phone from the pocket I'd been subtly trying to reach.

"Oh man," she said, showing the phone to Dorian and Coach Noonan. "We don't want him to have that!"

Uh-oh. I looked helplessly at Joe as my last ray of hope dissolved. *We can't let them put us in that warehouse,* I thought. Whatever David was or wasn't saying . . . I knew that once we went in, we'd never get out.

Joe looked away from me then, raised his bound wrists to his face, scratched his nose, and placed his hands back by his waistband—where he very, very subtly pointed. I looked where his finger landed and sucked in my breath.

He'd shoved the Taser in his waistband.

Then Joe reached up and tugged on his ear.

I knew what that meant.

Go time.

DANGER ZONE 16

JOE

I COULD SEE IN FRANK'S EXPRESSION THAT HE understood. I could also see that he wasn't at all confident that this was going to work. But I could also *also* see that he was my brother, and he trusted me, and we didn't have a ton of options trapped in a helicopter with four people who wanted to kill us.

Suddenly Frank jumped in his seat and began forcefully shaking, almost like he was having a seizure. "Oh God, oh God, oh God," he whimpered, "not now . . ." He moaned.

David whipped his head around, then back to the windshield. From the large buildings below us, I guessed that we were flying over Newport, which was a few towns over from Bayport. "What's happening?" he demanded.

"He's having a panic attack," I said. "He gets them sometimes."

Frank kept moaning. His eyes rolled up into his head.

"Guys, we have to do something!" I cried. "Sometimes they're so bad he stops breathing."

"What do I care?" David asked. But I could see Dorian, Kelly, and Coach Noonan exchange concerned looks.

"Let me get over there," Coach Noonan said tensely. "I took an emergency medicine class in college. I think I can help him."

Noonan was sitting on my right side. He quickly unclipped his seat belt and stood halfway, leaning over me to get to Frank.

I pulled the Taser from my waistband and shocked him.

"AAAAAAAUUUUUGH!" Coach Noonan yelled.

Things got chaotic for a minute, with Coach Noonan yelling, Kelly and Dorian screaming, and Frank miraculously recovering and trying to get out of the way. But when the smoke cleared, so to speak, I'd shocked Dorian too, and Frank had wrestled Kelly into the corner, where he was holding her.

I slipped my arms, still with the wrists bound, over David's head and pulled tight, nearly choking him.

"We can do this the easy way," I told him, "or the hard way."

"Let go of me!" David insisted.

But when he struggled and wasn't able to shake me off, I said again, "Easy way or hard way?"

He groaned. "What's the easy way?"

"You take us back to the baseball field at Waltham Park," I said. "The police should be waiting there."

"Are you crazy?" David scoffed. "I'm piloting this thing! Whatever thuggish game you're trying to play, I'm in charge. And there's no way I'm giving up that easily! You can do what you want to the others—I'm not letting you down anywhere but the ware—"

BZZZZZT.

I Tased him.

David slumped to the floor.

The helicopter lurched to the left.

Kelly screamed. "AAAAAAAAAAUGH! ARE YOU CRAZY?! We're all going to die!"

I looked at Frank. "Maybe not," I said, turning back to Kelly. "Do you have a pocketknife, or maybe a set of keys?"

She looked at me like I was out of my mind but produced a set of car keys. I grabbed them and quickly used them to poke through the duct tape binding Frank's hands.

"All right, bro," I whispered to him as the helicopter lurched sideways again. "There's no time to waste. Get in there!"

CRASH LANDING 17

FRANK

I HAVE A SECRET.

A secret is different from a dream. A secret is something you're not proud of doing, but maybe you're good at it, and maybe it gives you pleasure.

My secret is that I play a lot of video games.

I've actually been trying to cut back as of late. But up till a couple months ago, I was playing quite a bit, and the game I was the best at was 'Nam Helicopter Hero.

And I know it sounds like a stretch, but the real-life controls of the Bound Industries copter looked pretty similar to the digitized controls I'd used in 'Nam Helicopter Hero.

"Have a seat, Frank," Joe said, pushing David Bound's unconscious body aside.

I sat. First I leveled out the copter, and then I began

piloting us on a course to the south, back toward Toms River.

"Give me your phone, Kelly," I heard Joe say, and she must have passed it over, because I could hear my brother dialing.

"Yeah, hi, this is Joe Hardy. I called earlier, from Waltham Park in . . . ? Yeah, right. Well, listen, the crooks got us into the helicopter—yeah, I know, they were very strong—and I kind of Tased the pilot and now my brother is trying to fly the thing from his experience playing video games."

He paused.

"'Nam Helicopter Hero."

Pause.

"Yeah, it is very realistic. But listen, do you maybe have someone you could call who can help us land this thing? We're in kind of a pickle, I guess you'd say."

Pause.

"Oh great, thanks."

"IS THIS REALLY HAPPENING RIGHT NOW?" cried Kelly.

"Sit down," Joe told her. "You have to stay calm. Oh, okay, thank you. Here, Frank."

He held the phone to my ear.

"Hello?" I asked.

"Hi," a friendly female voice said. "Um, are you flying a helicopter right now? Could you use some assistance?"

"Yes, and yes, that would be very helpful," I replied politely.

"Okay, great," she said. "Um, why don't you start by telling me what you see. . . ."

About thirty minutes later, we came to a somewhat shaky landing on Bayport High School's football field.

As soon as the landing skids hit the ground, Kelly let out a yelp.

"Oh, thank God!" she cried. She jumped forward and then suddenly her arms were around my neck. "Thank you, thank you, thank you!"

"You know," Joe said, "you could have avoided that whole experience by *not* agreeing to do the bidding of some psycho."

Kelly glared at him. Joe ignored her and opened up the cockpit door.

Outside, we were greeted by bright flashing lights—police cruisers and three ambulances were waiting for our arrival. Two figures also stood silhouetted on the field: Principal Gerther and Dad.

As soon as Joe poked his head out, police officers and EMTs began swarming toward the helicopter.

"How many people are unconscious?" an EMT asked Joe.

"Three," Joe said, "and the girl in there who's conscious is also a bad guy, just to make that clear."

The EMT gave him kind of a funny look but pushed into

the cockpit anyway. I stood up from the controls. My legs felt hollow.

"Nice job, Frank," Joe said, clamping me on the shoulder. "I knew we could count on you!"

"Thanks," I said, smiling. We squeezed out of the copter and ran over to meet Dad and Principal Gerther.

"BOYS," said Principal Gerther. "I CAN'T TELL YOU HOW GRATEFUL I AM! IF I HAD KNOWN WHAT DASTARDLY PLANS THAT DAVID BOUND HAD IN STORE, I WOULD HAVE . . ." He trailed off.

"Principal Gerther," I said, "are you wearing your hearing aid?"

He looked surprised. "NO," he said, "I MUST HAVE FORGOTTEN. GOING TO TAKE SOME GETTING USED TO!"

I smiled and looked at Dad. "Is Owen all right?" I asked.

"If you mean the security guard," Dad said, "an ambulance took him to Bayport Memorial about half an hour ago. We've been told he's conscious and feeling as well as could be expected."

"Phew," I murmured.

"Principal Gerther," said Joe, turning to the principal with an uncomfortable look, "I have some bad news."

"WHAT'S THAT?" asked Gerther, looking beyond us to the helicopter.

Joe looked at me and winked. "If it's all right with you," he said, "I think we're ready to quit the basketball team."

18
A SOUND ENDING

JOE

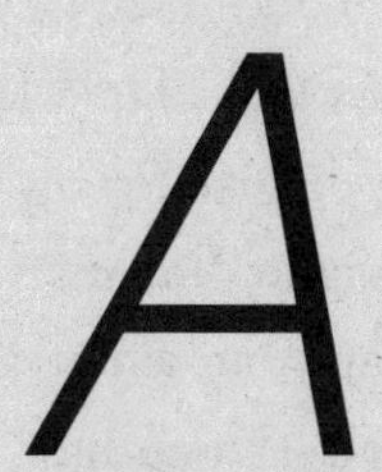

LL'S WELL THAT ENDS WELL.

Or so they say.

The Bayport High School Tigers couldn't quite recover from the aftershocks of David Bound's evil hazing plan being found out. Coach Noonan was fired, of course. Coach Perotta was placed on probation for failing to look into the hazing the first time it was reported, although a further investigation revealed that he truly seemed to have no knowledge of the hazing scheme—he just didn't want to believe something like that could happen on his team.

In the end, roughly half the varsity team was suspended for participating in the hazing. Steve, Gabe, Jayden, Pete, and Ty were all found to have no involvement.

More surprisingly, it turned out that Jason Bound himself was totally unaware of his father's crazy plans. Since he was close to Dorian, Dorian would sometimes learn that Jason had invited a teammate to meet up after practice, and use that as an opportunity to grab the kid for hazing.

But David was right. Jason was too *sportsmanlike* to actually be involved in such nonsense.

He came up to apologize to Frank and me at lunch about a week after the helicopter incident.

All eyes turned to the tall, popular senior as he weaved in between the tables of less popular kids in the back of the lunchroom, looking for us.

"Listen," he said as he approached us, "Joe and Frank, I don't even know what to say. How can I apologize for my dad's crazy actions? Or Kelly's, for that matter? We broke up, but clearly not soon enough."

"You don't have to apologize, Jason," I said honestly. "Your dad did crazy things—not you."

"I just wish I had known any of this was going on," he said, shaking his head. "I could have stopped it. So many guys got hurt 'cause of me!"

"But you didn't know that," said Frank kindly. "Listen, you can't control what other people do on your behalf. But I heard you get to keep the scholarship to Duke."

Jason nodded. "Yeah, even though we lost the championship."

Having half the team suspended, and one coach fired, isn't good for a team's performance, it seems.

"You played really well," I said. "Just . . . kill 'em in college."

Jason smiled. "You bet I will."

And then we were interrupted by the smooth strains of the band Chicago—sung a cappella.

Hold me now.
It's hard for me to say I'm sorry . . .

Frank's eyes lit up as suddenly, the a cappella group, the B-Sharps, began filing over to our table, surrounding it with glorious a cappella sound.

"Uh, gotta go," muttered Jason, and he was gone in a flash.

All eyes in the cafeteria were on our table as the B-Sharps serenaded Frank, really putting their all into the lyrics.

Personally? I just can't get that into a cappella.

But Frank looked like he'd died and gone to heaven.

When they finished, the cafeteria erupted in applause. But Max Crandal, the team captain, held up his hand for silence.

"Frank Hardy," he said, "the B-Sharps humbly ask for your forgiveness. We've heard all about how you helped shut down the hazing that was taking place on the basketball team. We now realize that when you bailed on our practices, it wasn't your choice. You were called to duty elsewhere."

"I was," agreed Frank.

Max nodded. "Frank, I accused you of not being right for the B-Sharps, but I realize now how lucky the B-Sharps were that you wanted to be one of us. Will you come back and join your brothers in a cappella harmony?"

Frank's eyes lit up. "*Will* I?" he asked, jumping up. "When do we perform again? And do I get the 'Lion Sleeps Tonight' solo back?"

"No," said Max, shaking his head. "Kyle is *killing* that solo, honestly. But we'll find something else for you."

Frank looked around at his a cappella brothers. He began singing, in a crazy-high falsetto . . .

And I'll take with me the memories
To be my sunshine after the rai-ai-ain . . .

They all joined in. I didn't know what song they were singing, but they all sure did. In one big clump, they began walking out of the cafeteria, my brother among them, singing his heart out. I dug into my daily special. I'd lost him.

But I wasn't too worried. After all, how often does a man get to live out his dream?

Besides, I was pretty sure another case would come along soon. Nothing brings the Hardy boys together like a good mystery.